Short Story

CENTERVILLE, U. S. A.

CENTERVILLE, U. S. A.

BY

CHARLES MERZ

Short Story Index

 BOOKS FOR LIBRARIES PRESS
FREEPORT, NEW YORK

First Published 1924
Reprinted 1971

INTERNATIONAL STANDARD BOOK NUMBER:
0-8369-3922-0

LIBRARY OF CONGRESS CATALOG CARD NUMBER:
78-160943

PRINTED IN THE UNITED STATES OF AMERICA

CONTENTS

CENTERVILLE, U. S. A.

There are more Centervilles in the United States than towns of any other name.

—*U. S. Census Reports.*

CENTERVILLE, U. S. A.

GRANDPA GILPIN

I

GRANDPA GILPIN had a birthday present. The family gave him a radio when he turned eighty-one.

No aërial appeared upon the roof. But that was n't Grandpa Gilpin's fault; he lived with May, his married daughter, and the house was not his own.

He was comfortable enough. The spare bedchamber up beneath the eaves, originally planned for a maid's room when the family fortunes marked a higher tide, was large enough to hold two chairs, a cot, a stone-topped wash-stand, and a chest of drawers.

Down-stairs, in the pantry, three good meals a day were ready for the asking. To be sure, eighty-one is none too certain of itself with fork and spoon; the stain of egg comes more easily from linoleum than linen; and some time had passed since May suggested to her father that it would be more convenient all around if he used the kitchen table.

Still, no one went to bed hungry in this house while May's husband could provide. Grandpa Gilpin always found a plate to fill before he climbed the stairs. Certainly with food and shelter he had little cause to feel dissatisfied. Not with a daughter in the house. And not for a traveler so far along the road as eighty-one.

Now and then, of course, it was a little lonely up beneath the eaves. May's husband came up-stairs at seven in the evening, to ask if it was warm enough or cool enough, and bring the morning paper from the city. The boys were always on their way to the movies or a call somewhere when they 'd come home from the mill and changed their clothes and finished supper. Grandpa Gilpin would hear them, one flight down, and wonder whose porch chairs they planned to rock to-night. Occasionally they 'd trudge up-stairs before they left, to tell him. May herself seldom missed a visit with her father in the morning. Of course she had her hands full. Cooking for six is work enough for any woman if she likes to get outside the house a little. May had her own friends and her interests. But she would climb the stairs for half an hour while the bread was baking or the wash was out to dry. She 'd bring her sewing with her, and rock in a chair while she told her father what a fortunate thing it was for all of them that Fred, her husband, was a frugal man and kept a roof above their heads. Could n't he (Grandfather Gilpin) be a little more considerate about venturing down-stairs? Those men last night were business friends, and had to have it explained to them afterward that nobody meant to speak unkindly when Fred asked Grandpa to go up-stairs again.

Sometimes, with May's visit in the morning, Fred's evening journey with the paper, and perhaps a few minutes with the youngest of the boys, Grandpa Gilpin found an hour of his day's twenty-four had worn itself away. There were a good many left untouched, however, when even eighty-one could not be sleeping. Grandpa Gilpin knew the shape and slope of every roof commanded by his dormer-windows; he knew the mail was heavy if the postman was so much as seven minutes late in going up the street; he knew how many times a day Miss

Murdock opened her kitchen door, came out
on the steps, sifted a dust-pan gently on the
ash-heap, went in and shut the door again.
The Gardner house, next door, was too close
to look down in the alleyway between; but
Grandfather Gilpin could tell the scrape of
the meat-man's feet on the top porch step
from the way the grocer tapped his shoes
against the rail, to clean them. One day
Miss Paulding, next to the church across
the street, received a telegram and must
have had to pay for it, she kept the boy so
long. Grandfather Gilpin used to sit on
his bed sometimes, and race his watch
against the brass tick of an alarm-clock
propped against the mirror.

Now and then he 'd lift his eyes, and the
square glass would show him a head that
rocked a little on its shoulders, as if he were
agreeing with himself in a series of little
never-ending nods. The doctors have a

name for that, but to Grandfather Gilpin it was just a way of holding up a head that was a little tired, now, at eighty-one. It was a good head, despite the hollows in the cheeks. Grandfather Gilpin saw a score of wrinkles deep enough to lay a finger in, but could not feel that he was really old. Eighty-one was well along, no doubt; some men might think it near the end. But Grandpa Gilpin could n't feel that way himself. Die? Certainly not yet. He felt himself too much a part of all this world around him. Where would Centerville have been without the Gilpins? Grandfather could remember when his brother John put up the first pine shanty west of Yellow River. He could remember the first string of heavy trucks that shook a wooden station with their rumble, the first cobblestones that turned Market Street from a pasture to a highway, the first spike driven for the interurban line whose crimson cars now woke the dead with their shrill whistles in the night.

Gilpin had been a name to conjure with, in Centerville. These brothers were a family of pioneers. Grandpa Gilpin knew that a man might find it difficult to keep up with things. But it was a little strange, he thought, that no one came to ask for his opinion. Changes every day; all right enough and all wise enough, may be. But the town went on without him.

II

The radio was an inspiration. Not only for the new interest which it brought upstairs, but for the peace and comfort given to the giver.

May's husband brought it home one night: a set that had seen better days. One of the bulbs refused to light, and the secondary coil had suffered from some mishap; but the man who brought it to the store declared it could be fixed without much trouble, and volunteered to trade it for a bill that he 'd been owing. May's husband did n't want it for himself. He was a God-fearing man who liked his evenings quiet. But he had brought it home, for all that, wrapped in the same newspaper package in which it came to him.

"What on earth will you do with it?" May had asked him. "You *know* you won't let anything disturb you after supper. Why, if one of the boys starts whistling——"

"I know," May's husband said. "I don't intend to use it. I thought we 'd take it up to Grandpa."

"But Grandpa *will* use it, if you give it to him," May had pointed out. "And you

know how thin the walls are. Every time
he moves you can hear him creak around.
He 'll make life miserable for all of us if
you let him have that thing."

"He can't do that," her husband told her.
"It 's broken, for one thing. And anyway
I think you can fix it so you have to use
ear-phones. Besides, we have n't even got
one of those things on the roof to bring the
waves in."

"Then what 's the use of giving it to
him?"

"Well, it 's something he can play with."

"Will you have it fixed?"

"I don't think so."

"Then will you tell him it won't work?"

"No," Fred replied. "He 'd just get
tired of it anyway. And he might as well
think there 's something in it, while his interest lasts. It 'll keep him busy for a

while. The important thing is to keep him up there in his room a little more. You know what I mean."

Unquestionably, that was the important thing. For ever since Grandfather Gilpin had an attack of vertigo on Maple Street and fell across the low fence around Willis Bender's lot so limp and tired that it was an hour before they dared bring him home again, the family had realized that no longer could he tour the streets without some one to watch him. That meant the day indoors; for who had time to putter to the corner at Grandfather Gilpin's pace, to see if Martin Deane had burned his pile of autumn leaves or the potatoes in the grocery window had given way to corn and beans? Barred from access to the streets, Grandpa Gilpin took to prowling through the house. And that brought a series of misfortunes in its train.

There was the day when, dizzy for a mo-

ment at the mantelpiece, Grandpa Gilpin
caught a friendly piece of scrollwork that
seemed to have been put there for just such
a purpose, and took away with him the
whole upper deck of shelves and treasured
vases when he stumbled to the couch.
There was the day, not two weeks afterward, when May—whose pleasures in the
day's routine were few enough and far between—was mortified to have a meeting of
her card club interrupted by Grandfather
Gilpin in his shirt-sleeves, collar open at
the throat, a wash-basin in his hands—stray-
ing in amid the guests, blue eyes alight with
interest, to display an unexpected and important crack. There was another day,
May's husband said, when he might have
sold the largest single order of the season to
a business man from out of town, had not
Grandfather Gilpin, at the worst moment
to be chosen, come stumbling in to ask if

any one had noticed that the Dorners had their screens off for the winter and another month or two might bring a late fall snow. By the time Grandfather Gilpin had been sent to bed again, the hour was late, there was a train arriving, and the business man from out of town was on his way with nothing left behind him save a promise he would think things over.

"I don't want to be unkind," May's husband told the family next day at supper, "but he 's got to know that other people in the house have rights beside himself. He 's getting worse each day."

"Why don't you try that radio and see what it 'll do?" the second son suggested. "Give it to him Friday. Mother 's been saying that 's his birthday."

"Won't do any harm," agreed May's husband. "It may keep him interested for a little while. I don't know what 's going to be the end of this. I 've been a patient man for many years, but I 'll tell you! when things go on this way, day after day——"

And so Grandpa Gilpin got a birthday present.

III

The wonders of science never cease. No man can predict its ultimate achievement. For two months Grandpa Gilpin had had his radio; and long after dark he would sit there fumbling with the three strange knobs and listening for an answer.

Eyes that had been watching life for four score years were still keen—how many men at eighty-one could count the shingles on a neighbor's roof, a good sixty feet and more away?—but ears were another matter. Grandpa Gilpin did n't catch as much as he would like to, and so he sat down very close upon this gift of his that brought the world back into his own life again. A great invention, he was sure—but a great invention still some way from perfect. For certainly it seemed to him a long time between reverberations in the air. Only once did noise break suddenly upon his rapt attention. That was on a day when the Burkes, next door, had bought themselves a phonograph. The street was quiet. It was an afternoon well toward the end of fall; but warm enough, May thought, to have the windows open in the hall.

Grandpa Gilpin stumbled to the kitchen stairs, that day, and in his thin high voice piped to his daughter:

"May! It's started coming! Music, May! Come up! Just think, right here at home—and them 'way off—why, mebbe a thousand miles and more! Who'd ever 've thought I'd see this day? John wouldn't 've believed it!—May! ain't you coming up?"

One triumph, in a vigil of two months. Next day it was colder. May had the windows closed. One triumph: a slim reward for amateurs without much time to spare. But time was Grandpa Gilpin's great possession.

Head turned sideways to the friendly horn, eyes fixed on a chart of station calls: he would spin those three round knobs that caught the ether by its heels.

Down-stairs, peace and quiet reigned.

Up-stairs, underneath the eaves, a spent man with a spent machine was reaching for a world that lives and breathes.

COD MACY

I

THE whole town used to say Cod Macy ought to be deported. His presence on the scene was a disgrace. His chief offense, and incidentally his staff of life, was not a subject to be shouted from the house-tops; but Centerville observed that the sport coupé, the permanent wave in Mrs. Macy's auburn hair, and the oil-burning furnace in the Macy cellar, all dated since the days of Andrew Volstead.

There was n't a man in Centerville with a good word to say for Cod. "Ought to put that fellow on a freight-car," old Judge Whipple would declare, "and ship him clear

across the country. No place too far away
for him."

"That's right, Judge," the town would
say. "No place too far away."

And yet, even in those days before a hint
of reformation had appeared, Cod Macy's
lot was not the hard life of a social outcast.
If you had walked with him down Market
Street some afternoon, you'd not have
found the whole town treating him as
though he were a moral leper. Sam War-
ner, struggling with an overcoat, would appear upon the threshold of Frye's barber
shop. As like as not, he'd just been telling
his fellow-customers inside that Cod deserved a lynching. But would this indignation still abide with him out here? No.
Sam would greet this culprit as a man
might greet a long-lost brother. "Well,
well! Who have we here? Cod Macy, as
I live! How's business, stranger?"

It would be much the same with Ira Niles and Captain Sampson Dodd, a few blocks farther down the street. Even old Judge Whipple lacked a measure of that disapproval manifested in a crowd. Cod would spy Judge Whipple first.

"Hi, Judge! What price you quoting justice?"

The Judge was fairly cautious. But if Market Street was not too crowded, he would sometimes halt a moment at the curb.

"Howdy, Cod," he would reply. "Er— by the way——"

Centerville, you see, was too small a neighborhood to live on terms of comfortable hostility even toward its villains. Moreover, if the truth be told, there was a certain fraction of the town—how large or small a fraction you may guess yourself— that looked to Cod to wrest it from the toils of Prohibition. It took a man of more than average daring to turn his back upon the source of all supply—and cut him dead on Market Street. Suppose the source retaliated then, by putting up his prices? This was no case in which to take a charge of trade discrimination to the courts.

The result was this: that though Cod Macy might be hanged in effigy wherever good men gathered on the hearth, it was not so easy to be done with him in public. He found a certain welcome on the streets. And being a congenial soul he picked the best streets and the busy hours. Market Street at half-past four on any Saturday revealed a sequence of embarrassed buyers sidling into open doors.

Cod Macy's progress at such times was little short of regal.

II

He was a small man, this lord of the

underworld in Centerville—with a box-like
face and a skin like Mocha coffee.   It was
his eyes that focused your attention.   Perhaps sometime you 've seen a children's puzzle with two small ball-bearings in a dish.   A
glass lid covers them.   You try to roll both
balls until they rest in little concave sockets.
One ball slips in.   The other hovers on the
crater's edge.   You shake it gently, lest you
rouse its colleague from repose.   It hes-
itates.   Then   plunges.   Whereupon   the
first one breaks away again—starts charging noisily around the saucer.   If you have
played that game you 've had the same sen-
sation you would get by standing at a distance of two feet, to look Cod Macy in the
eye.

And yet, for all that, he had a certain
frankness if you met him on his ground.
Anson Todd discovered that.   Anson Todd
was pastor of the Vine Street Church, and

one of Cod's respected neighbors. The two would stand at the garden fence sometimes, to trade opinions.

"Parson, how do you keep your roses from being chewed by bugs, the way they 've chewed up mine?" And Cod would roll his little bullet eyes around their saucers, and look off dimly at the trellis: as if there were something in this question bugs on bushes ought not hear, and he would make it easier for the parson with his answer.

But Anson Todd was not the man to speak of caterpillars peacefully when he felt he had a soul to save; and so—when they had talked of spraying powder on the rose-leaves, and hanging strips of paper so they 'd flutter in the wind and keep the birds from lighting on the aster beds and digging out the seeds—he would come to the point of his concern with that directness which had never failed him.

"Mr. Macy, you may say it 's no affair of mine; but I have heard some things about your business that alarm me."

"My business!" Cod would roll his eyes at this, until it seemed that never would those two ball-bearings be returned to their small sockets. "You mean my real estate?"

"No. I 'm told your real estate is quite fictitious, Mr. Macy. I 'm told it would be more the truth to say your business—shall I put it frankly?—is selling contraband supplies of gin and whisky."

"Well, as I live! You 've heard *that,* have you?" Mr. Macy would brush a bit of thistle from his coat lapel, and put his eyes in rapid transit round his face. There were various attitudes a man accused might take at such a juncture. Disbelief. An attitude of "Come! you 're joking." Indignation. Cod Macy sometimes let the pastor have a chance to win his case.

"I'm not saying, mind you, that what you've heard is true—or anything but gossip. Lord help me—no offense intended, parson—what stories *don't* you hear? This town just talks and talks and talks. Let a fellow make a little money, on his real estate, and right away they get their hatchets out. . . . But suppose you're right. Suppose I make my living selling what you call contraband. What about it?"

"No man in that position," Anson Todd would say, "can serve his church or be a useful citizen."

"I don't know about the first," Cod Macy would reply. "But now you take the second. Do I dodge my taxes or my jury duty? Do I meddle in town politics? Am I like these fellows who talk a lot but never vote? I've never missed a chance to vote in all my life. And let me tell you, I never fail to mark my ballot for the drys."

"I 've no doubt of all that, Mr. Macy. In fact, in fairness I 'll say more. I know who it was, last year, who started a Christmas budget for families out of work. I know who slipped a twenty-dollar gold piece into my church platter, Easter Sunday. And I know you 're a good neighbor in more ways than one. But look at the other side of it, Mr. Macy. Here 's a friendly little town that never knew what it was, before, to break the law. You 've taught it how—if what they say is true. There 's nothing in your trade that is n't stealthy. There 's far more petty plotting, up and down the length of Market Street, to-day. Far more suspicion of one's neighbors. Far more disrespect for law. Far more——"

"And what do you think?" Mr. Macy would cut in. "Suppose I *am* this fellow you 're describing. Suppose I 'm *in* this trade. Suppose I quit. What happens?"

"If you want to know what I really think: one less sinner to be saved."

"And one less dealer in the market! Do you think if I dropped out of this—supposing I was in it—all these things you talk about would stop? Not for a minute! In no time there 'd be a fellow from the city here, to take my place. You 'll talk, I suppose, about my taking money that ought to buy the baby shoes. Well, let me tell you these city fellows would take the money that buys a whole lot else besides. They 'd boost the prices. They 'd bring in a lot of poisonous stuff that would kill somebody just as sure as you 're alive. And the same folks would keep on buying it. I *know*. Thank God nobody can say—or *could* say, if I went in for this sort of thing —that I ever sold a man rank poison.

"Oh, no," Cod Macy would wind up,

"you would n't find things different.   Just
worse.   It 's bad enough, I dare say, to shift
a pastor on the job—when a town gets used
to him.   But let me tell you that is n't anything compared to shifting a bootlegger
when you know he 's safe.

"You ask some of your vestrymen.
They 'll tell you."

III

The Rev. Anson Todd was no man to
leave a job half finished.   When rose-
petals withered, and the garden conversa-
tions got around to raking maple-leaves, he
suggested that no man whose conscience
troubled him had ever found the road to
peace.   When leaves were piles of ashes in
the street, and the present problem was the
proper way of storing window-screens, he
pointed out that Saul himself had been

converted in good season. Not for a moment did his interest slacken in the chase. With data culled from columns in the city press—crime waves and slipping morals—he confronted Mr. Macy at the garden fence. He borrowed Mr. Macy's garden tools. He urged his wife to cultivate an interest in the Macy lady.

That was no achievement to be rated lightly. Mrs. Macy was an Amazon: a tall woman with bright copper hair and a shrill voice that could be heard from Parson Todd's own windows, in the summer-time, complaining at the supper-table if the peas were burned. From the day the Macys moved to Centerville, four years or so ago, the town had viewed her as a problem. She had a way of swooping down on neighbors when she spied them in the streets, and sharing household gossip in a voice that carried to the corner. Centerville believed in live

and let live.   But it fled from Mrs. Macy
as it fled the sting of death.   In the end she
had given up pursuit of social standing, and
turned her back upon the town.

It was then that the wife of Anson Todd
had sought her out, and for want of an alternative undertaken to arouse her interest
in a church bazaar.   Mrs. Macy met this
offer with alacrity.   She issued from re-
tirement, swooped back on Centerville again,
and within two weeks had taken charge of
all arrangements.   They could n't think of
holding *this* bazaar, she said, in some one's
empty store-room.   They would hire Woodmen's Hall.   Her husband would be glad
to pay the charges as his contribution.
They 'd have cakes and ices from the city.
A little thing.   Her husband.   They would
have a church bazaar the likes of which the
town had never seen before.

Cod Macy thought his wife was making

much ado about a small affair, but gave it
his approval.   He was busy, now, with the
salting down of a new "shipment."   Cod
catered to the country-side for a dozen miles
around.   His produce came by motor from
the city, forty miles away.   Part of it was
canned in ancient maple-syrup tins.   Part
of it was bottled.   All of it was bad.   It
consisted usually of gin for which "syn-
thetic" was a mildly graphic term—of
Scotch that may have started in the High-
lands but showed signs of having picked up
new ingredients along the way.   All this
was raw material.   It remained for Cod to
take the thrice diluted, and dilute it more.

His wife helped, usually.   Too busy now,
he found her, with her church affairs.   There
were quarts and pints and stacks of old familiar labels to be pasted on the flanks of
flagons never gummed before.   "Bottled
1898" would still be wet with printer's ink

when it was pasted on a glass container blown in 1923. Scotch that was known as Black and White ten miles one side of Centerville changed into Haig and Haig ten miles the other. Impressive, what could be accomplished with a strip of green and yellow paper. Cod Macy had three patrons who insisted on Kentucky Bourbon —three others who preferred Virginia Rye. They got it. Poured with the same dipper from the same mellow maple-syrup can.

Not a business, you observe, that demanded rare administrative genius once you held the inside track. Orders flowed in largely of their own accord. The trade had no dull seasons.

"Say, Cod, I was thinking the other day —I was wondering—say, Cod, I was just thinking the other day maybe you could tell me how to get a little—well, *you* know——"

Wife not well? Brother coming for an

unexpected visit? Sister's doctor thought she ought to have a tonic? . . . Cod Macy's training led him to this observation:

That the longer the preamble, when a man set out to buy, the firmer his reputation as a pillar of society—and the shorter the order, when it came.

IV

With Anson Todd, the argument went on—across the garden fence. Fall turned to winter: the problem now was how to keep an ice-crust off the sidewalk with a garden-spade. Winter got along to spring: time to put the zinnias in their beds and move the cherry-tree before the sap began to run. Cod Macy had n't budged from his position. Against all argument of press and pulpit he stood firm. But it was clear to Anson Todd that something new was trou-

bling him. Conscience, said the parson.
Cod knew better. Not conscience, but his
wife.

She was launched, now, upon that recovery of social prestige to which a brilliant
administration of the church bazaar, followed in swift succession by a hard times
ball and a Christmas fête, entitled her.
She would come home tired, to narrate the
story of the day's adventures:

"Mrs. Martin Deane is *such* a pleasant
woman. . . . *Her* husband 's in the clothing
trade."

Or: "The Women's Literary Club is
going to meet at Mrs. Arthur Gregg's this
afternoon. Of course I don't belong to it.
They 've never asked me. Mrs. Gregg is
very cordial since we did our work for the
bazaar. But of course *her* husband is a
banker."

It dawned gradually upon Cod Macy that

if peace of mind were any asset, he was guilty of an indiscretion when he blessed the church bazaar. His wife was off: there seemed no stopping her. In vain he took her to the city for a week-end round of gaieties: "We must be getting back," she told him. "They may be planning something else, and of course they would n't save a place for me."

He built a porch across his house. His wife had always wanted one.

"It will be lovely to have it when June comes," she agreed. "But then, of course, we have n't as much use for porches as *some* people have."

"Why have n't we?"

"We don't have many visitors," she said. And sighed.

He took the proceeds of a record-breaking shipment of Virginia Rye—or Kentucky Bourbon, if you choose—and brought her home a bracelet from Wade's jewelry store.

"It's a *beauty,* dear!" she said. "I saw it in the window just a day or two ago. Mrs. Case and I admired it. She has *such* good taste, you know. Her husband is an architect."

Patience has its limits. Cod Macy exploded into indignation at this point. "Good taste? Husband is an architect, is he? Yes. And what does he *get* by being one, I'd like to know! A miserable little fee or two—that's what he gets. A miserable little fee or two—after he's stood around, and begged awhile, and got some plumber to feel sorry for him. . . . An architect, is he? Well, I'd like to see *him* bring home a bracelet like that for his wife! I'd like to see *him* run a house the way we do, and keep a car, and buy his wife fur coats. . . . An architect, eh? Just tell me what it gets him!"

There are smiles one gives a child who means well, but who does n't understand. Mrs. Macy shook her head. "There are other things in the world," she told her husband, "than mere money."

Cod Macy stood at the garden fence one night, and rolled his eyes so briskly that across the fence his neighbor felt fresh news was on its way.

"I 've been thinking over the things you 've told me, parson. I 've been thinking over all you 've told me, and some other things. And to tell the truth, I bought out Andrew Marshall's lumber trade to-day. I 'm going to give up certain—certain interests on the side."

Anson Todd reached across the fence and took his neighbor's hand.

"Yes, I 'm in the lumber trade from now on," Cod continued. "I 'm in the lumber trade, and I want to be known to everybody as a lumber man."

"Mr. Macy,'" said the parson, "you have given me new faith. For any influence my words have had, I am profoundly grateful."

Cod Macy gripped the hand held out to him, and rolled his eyes. Next week the village had a building boom.

HENRIETTA CROSBY

I

THEY used to say that Yellow River had an undertow. And certainly to stay out after curfew rang was a challenge flung at the police. But for most lads nine or ten years old these terrors struck a minor note. It was Henrietta Crosby of whom small boys were apt to dream when they had eaten too much turkey: Henrietta Crosby, ruler poised alertly in one hand, demanding whether Fujiyama was a river or a mountain.

Tall, narrow-shouldered, as angular as that sharp-cornered field which A and B had planned to plant with winter wheat, in Wentworth's "Introduction to Arithmetic"

39

—Miss Crosby towered high above the desk that held the famous ruler in its left-hand drawer. Her face was thin; her gray hair combed straight down across her temples like two curtains parted at a window-pane. She did n't often smile; and when she did, her lips stayed stiff—as if they needed practice. Her eyes were either green or gray; it was hard telling which, behind the thick glass lenses that protected them. But whether they were green or whether they were gray, there was nothing wrong with their perception. The boys in the last row could testify that they were strong enough to look straight through her head and catch a furtive note half-way across the aisle.

The last row had good reason to be cautious. The flock viewed its shepherd with a lively fear. History, arithmetic, geography, and grammar: Miss Crosby attacked them with a missionary's zeal. No trifling with the rules of syntax—no hit-or-miss impressions of the world; either the Marne poured itself into the Seine, or the Seine poured itself into the Marne: you could not satisfy her with the statement both were rivers. Precision was the goal at which she aimed; she spared no effort to attain it. No other teacher in the schools of Centerville imposed so frequently the penalty of "staying after school"—or displayed, in her choice of afternoons, a genius so completely fatal. Martin Sales defined the Ganges as a glacier—and the fourth grade, in its most important contest of the season, lost its center fielder.

II

One class followed on another's heels. When the center fielder's mother was a banner pupil in the grades, Henrietta Crosby had n't won her reputation as a tyrant.

She was younger then, of course; younger by some twenty years. Her hair was brown instead of gray; her lips were better used to smiling. Still, it was n't years that made the difference; "ask Miss Crosby," was a byword for young men of nine or ten when the sky was dark and the world seemed lost in trouble. There was n't a better friend to intercede with the angry owner of a window broken by a baseball. There was n't a teacher more intent on overlooking little indiscretions, days when circus came to town. There was n't an enthusiast who made as much ado about a holiday. Arbor day the fourth-grade walls would be hung with green and white—and green and red at Christmas. Pumpkins on the desk, Thanksgiving week. Miss Crosby would come down from her dais to mingle with an audience of parents; young voices filled the room with "Woodman, spare that tree," and the schooner *Hesperus* ran to her destruction with the gale. The school would sing "It came upon the Midnight Clear" while parents did their best to accept congratulations modestly, and shower praise on other parents' sons. Always there were prizes. Not useless things like catechisms and embroidered mottos for a mother's wall; but catcher's mitts and ribbons for young ladies' hair.

Certainly this was another Henrietta Crosby. Had the change come suddenly, or just sifted down with time? Things like that are n't written in the record. No one remembered, now; but a host of parents knew that for three years at least the fourth grade had been made to tremble. A few of Henrietta Crosby's older friends ascribed the difference to her sister.

Not that there was anything here to explain affairs precisely. The sister had been on the scene to work her mischief, not for three years, but a dozen. Still, it was possible—these friends of Henrietta Crosby said—that she had just begun to feel the burden. That might account for her high-handedness. Plainly it was nerves, they said. The sister was a problem.

She was a younger sister. Years ago she 'd gone away from Centerville, and marched with triumph through the city schools. In the old days Henrietta Crosby boasted of Louise. Never, she declared, had there been a girl more certain to achieve great things. The career was nipped with frost before it had a chance to blossom. A long illness left the sister paralyzed; they brought her home, an invalid.

Even Henrietta Crosby's most thorough-going critics, provided they were not base-ball captains losing heavy-hitting center fielders in a pinch, admitted she had made a gallant struggle. The sister never left her bed. Henrietta Crosby was a slave to the simplest facts of her existence; she lived two lives as best she could, and fought to keep from flying off the handle. With a sense of injustice pardonable, perhaps, in an invalid bedridden with all life before her, the sister grew more irritable, more exacting, more convinced that all the cruelty of the ages had been piled upon her narrow bed. Henrietta Crosby had no problem so simple as A and B debating how many furrows a foot and a half apart would plow their field for barley.

Nor was that all. Courage might keep a grip on health and reason; but courage had small part to play in keeping house. These sisters lived on Henrietta's eight-hundred-dollar salary, and made it do for two. Henrietta Crosby was well on toward sixty now; years in the galley had left their mark. There was no telling how much longer she could go. One beacon beckoned through the shadows: two more years of service meant a pension.

No problem in the works of Wentworth put a greater premium on time.

III

The Crosbys were a tight-lipped lot. It was old Miller Crosby who had died without admitting to his doctor that he had a jumpy heart. Henrietta had her father's curtness. She did n't take her troubles to the town. Most people knew there was a crippled sister; not more than half a dozen knew the rest. Henrietta might have made a more successful bid for sympathy if she had tried. Still, there were no friends stanch enough to take her side at school; her pupils had no hand in this. The thing was scarcely fair; to visit on their heads the troubles she stored up at home was carrying things too far.

No doubt the fourth grade had a time of it. Miss Crosby grew more unapproachable from day to day, and more eccentric. There seemed to be no explanation for her whims. She had given up all oral recitations. Everything was written now. "A buys six bushels of potatoes at forty cents a peck. He sells them to B at a profit of two dollars—" Miss Crosby would write her questions on the blackboard in a firm round hand. When there were eight or ten of them the class would get its tablets out, and puzzle for the answers. Even spelling took its turn on tablets now. No more of the line that used to reach across the platform, with all honor to the lad who held his place the longest. Nowadays Miss

Crosby read her words from the pages of
Cyr's "Fourth Reader" in a thin dry
voice—"pasturage," "shepherd," "sinewy,"
"thither," "olive"—and the words came back
to her on paper.

Any sort of conversation seemed to worry
her. People noticed that, outside of school.
It had been so long since she first hurried
by her neighbors with a distant nod that
even the most friendly and the most inquisi-
tive had given up attempts to stop her.
Merchants sent their clerks to wait on her,
when she invaded Market Street. She
was a shopper difficult to handle—quick-
tempered, obstinate in her demands, paying
no attention to what people told her. Malcolm Ross, who ran a shoe store near the
railway-station, used to say he took to cover
when he saw her at the door. Always expecting her to pounce on him, he said, with
"what 's the capital of Ecuador?"—and give

him two more pairs of shoes to cobble before supper if he did n't know the answer.

Still, what happened in the shops and on the streets was not a matter of importance. There were plenty of other people there, ready enough to talk, and plenty who could be made to listen if they had to. It was within the blackboard walls of Henrietta Crosby's room that silence took its toll. A school without an echo is a cheerless place. Arbor days went by without a celebration now. It had been a long time since the blackboards heard the clattering hoofs of Paul Revere.

The school had no more prizes; no more consultations at its teacher's desk—with plans about to-morrow's work, and shy requests for special favors. Miss Crosby had discouraged that. Ten is a likely age for pelting questions at an older friend; Miss Crosby plainly showed she did n't care for

friendship.   With petty tyrannies, and pun-
ishment that outweighed crime, she warned
her pupils there would be no quarter.   Her
reputation ran ahead of her.   When some
scholar more intrepid than his schoolmates
stayed to ask a question, she did n't seem to
listen—shook her head, and glared until he
went away.

Silence in her class-room.   She lived behind a wall.   Silence, and a flash of temper
when some pupil tried to cross the line of her
reserve.

You might have thought that Henrietta
Crosby was tired hearing voices.

IV

Supper had been cooked, the dishes
washed, a vain effort made to soothe her sister's bitter pride.   Henrietta Crosby sat in

the darkened room in which this invalid of
hers proclaimed each night brought rest
more tortured, and from a low chair at the
window watched the quiet street.

It was a warm night in early fall; a new
school term had started.   She was thinking
of a lad with curly hair who had n't seemed
to know that in this school of his he faced
an ogre.   He had the first seat in the second
row; lots of other youngsters had struggled with their A's and B's at that low
desk in years before him.   Not one, in all
of Henrietta Crosby's twenty-three, a lad
with cheeks a redder red or smile more
friendly.

He had come to her when the day was
over, and put a small red dirty hand upon
her desk, and looked at her with parted
lips and shining eyes—as if he had the
greatest of all secrets to be shared.   What

would he have said, if she had let him
speak—and not frowned at him and nodded
at the door? Some feat, performed that
very day, that rivaled deeds of Hercules?
Some treasure found, in the damp recesses
of a vacant lot, more wonderful than any
buried gold of Captain Kidd's?

Her arms had wanted to reach out around
this boy—to draw him close—to hold him
on her knee.

Absurd of her, to think of doing that.
In a moment they would know the story.
Two more years, she had; two more years
before the pension came. They'd never
let her have them, if they knew.

No. There was one way. She'd chosen
it.

The low chair was rocking at the window.
Henrietta Crosby watched the quiet street.
How late? she thought.

Down-stairs a clock had hammered out

its strokes with heavy hands. But Henrietta Crosby was n't used to hearing clocks.

Stone-deaf. She had n't heard a whisper in three years.

DOCTOR HODGE

I

SIXTY-SIX is well along in life to take on extra burdens. But Simon Hodge's friends declared bad luck had left him looking ten years younger. He carried on the torch alone.

There was n't a more familiar figure on the scene in Centerville. Everybody knew him; everybody loaded trouble on his shoulders. He was a semi-private, semi-public institution like the bank. He had a young assistant for a time. But in his older patients' eyes that young assistant scarcely counted; for anything more serious than chicken-pox or measles, everybody wanted Doctor Hodge himself. What small portion of the town he had not personally helped bring into the world, and wrapped in swaddling-clothes, he had subsequently patched for broken limbs or argued with for gout.

You would see his weather-beaten Ford pull up against the curb and choke its motor; then the man himself climb out, start up the walk, remember he had left his bag, turn back again to get a battered satchel. All Centerville was interested in health, especially its neighbors'. Nothing else aroused more comment than a new illness up the street, or a sudden complication in an old one. Cities have nothing of the sort to draw upon, for civic interest. The whole town knew the intimate details of Arthur Day's new diet—of Newton Smith's recovery from tonsilitis—of Ned Frye's stubborn battle with lumbago. "Mrs. Meigs's heart-trouble must be getting worse," the banker or the butcher or the parson would tell his wife at supper. "I see Doc Hodge's car stop there this morning."

"Stopped again, did he? How long this time?"

"Well, he was gone when I came back around the corner. Still, it looked like it might be something serious. I noticed that the Doc took both bags with him to the house."

Everybody knew, before the day was over, where Simon Hodge had stopped, how long he stayed, and what was probably the answer.

Everybody knew, too, the six straight chairs in Hodge's waiting-room—the reading-matter on his table, headed by the State Survey of Roads. A poor place to wait for anything, especially for news that might be bad. Still, even in this barren spot an all-absorbing interest in one's neighbor's illness never slackened; patients sat their turn on these stiff chairs and carried on a lively barter in their symptoms.

Farther on, beyond the door that creaked a warning when it sought another volunteer, the inner office opened up a dimly lighted shrine. At the window, catching what small sunshine bent around the wall outside, a walnut desk bowed down beneath a load of half-forgotten papers; on the wall, an ancient telephone with nickel-plated eyes and long retroussé nose; then a small enamel basin gurgling with a stream of water—a row of dusty text-books slowly parting with their backs—a skeleton that looked a little weird at night, when its lean ribs caught the unexpected glint of an electric light; but rather amiable by day—loose jaws overhanging in a friendly simper.

In one corner of the room a case of surgeon's implements, from which the doctor borrowed freely, to make repairs upon his Ford and help him with odd chores around the garden. More than one pair of scissors made to slit an epigastrium had gone to clip unruly branches in the yard.

II

Tall, white-haired, well on the road to seventy, Hodge had been writing the same old-fashioned remedies in a dog-eared prescription book for more than forty years. Two things his patients noted. First his hands: long fingers, trembling slightly, but still admirably nimble in their trade. Then his eyes: brown eyes, badly focused, looking on expectantly for something they had never seen. Born in another day, the chances are that Simon Hodge would have followed some crusader's flag or sailed a frigate on the Spanish Main. Perhaps it takes a man like that to be a small-town doctor.

Certainly Simon Hodge was as poor a hand at business as those eyes made him out to be. "Sick?" he would say, to some patient who might have been carried profitably on the books for several weeks. "Nonsense! *You're* not sick. It's just imagination." If income is man's goal in life, this doctor missed the major portion of his chances. Not only did he bar the door to patients till they furnished overwhelming proof that they were ill; once cured, he shipped them off as promptly and as finally as an indignant father in a melodrama might disown a wayward son. And worse than that, he never sent out bills.

Not that it was a matter of philanthropy with him. He thoroughly believed in bills. Periodically he resolved to set his books in order. But he had been resolving that for thirty years. He wrote his memoranda on bits of envelope and wrapping paper: "Mrs. Jones, one call, $1"—nothing more; no evidence which one of several Mrs. Joneses was intended; no inkling of a date or reason why. "Lady over Caldwell's Grocery, two calls for tonsilitis." Memoranda of that sort clogged one drawer of Simon Hodge's desk. The lady over Caldwell's had long since moved to nobler quarters; Simon Hodge had made a dozen sets of resolutions. But the day of judgment never came. He lived on what small tribute patients paid him of their own free will.

Or did—until the young assistant came.

III

They lived, the Hodges, in a small frame house on Market Street that might have been more comfortable if Simon Hodge liked keeping books. It was cramped and inconvenient, and from the shingles of its ancient roof to the untamed furnace in its soggy cellar cried aloud in every beam and radiator-valve for renovation. Hodge spent lots of hours drawing plans on back of envelopes, to show the way he meant to do it over. There would be a sun-porch here— and a roof that drooped, instead of sagged, in a pleasant curve to meet the doorway. Good plans; but Simon had been drawing something of the sort since his elder son was young enough to break an attic window with a baseball. And now both boys had moved away; both boys had families of their own; and still a shingle rattled in the broken window. Simon Hodge and his wife Mary lived in Maple Street alone.

She was a cherub, Mary—a cherub at sixty-five: round, red-cheeked, even-

tempered—as much in love with her husband, still, as any woman would have to be
to submit for thirty years to the savage
back-fire of a kitchen range that needed
piping in three places. Winter found her
tucking flannel into window-panes that
Simon Hodge had promised her, each year,
would not be there to rattle when another
Christmas came. Summer found her in the
garden. She liked the garden. Simon
liked it, too. It was the only spacious thing
about the house in Maple Street. Simon
liked the garden. It had n't any worries.
He could n't say as much about this young
man who 'd come to work with him.

They had put him up, when he first came
to town, in the spare bedroom that was only
a little drafty when the wind blew. There
was no doubt of Simon's needing him.
Sixty-six is sixty-six; there was plenty of
work to handle; and of course no man goes

on forever. Time to look for a successor, Simon told his wife; this lad might be the man. He arrived well recommended by his university: a young fellow of twenty-seven, with hard round cheeks and a gravity not to be disturbed by sudden sallies. He had finished his class-room work a bare three months before—and with him, now, he brought a tireless respect for science.

Simon Hodge had made a note of that even before he'd taken his assistant to the office, or had him at the bedside of a friend. They were sitting at supper, his first night in town, and the younger man was picturing a scene of horror. "Just imagine, doctor," he declared, "this surgeon I've been telling you about was so old-fashioned that he'd leave his needles on the desk, where they could gather dust. Can you imagine such a thing in this day and generation?"

With one corner of his eye Simon Hodge

could catch a glimpse of a small black case with its cover open, on a corner of the sideboard. Come to think of it, it was just that afternoon he 'd sewed a football for the boy across the garden fence.

"Well, well," he said, "you 'd scarcely think it, would you?"

He crossed the room to the sideboard; the black case disappeared. With a pitcher in his hands Doctor Hodge approached the supper-table. "Have some cider, doctor."

That was the start of it—but as Simon Hodge was fated to observe, by no means the end. This young man had scarcely been in town a week before the office lost its old-time ease. "Doctor, you 'll forgive me," he would say, "but *surely* you 've lost the glass covers for your bandage-trays. Of course you don't expose them to the air this way."

Simon Hodge would swear that the glass covers had been there no longer ago than yesterday, and had somehow disappeared; two antiseptic glass containers would be ordered from the city shops by mail. But one triumph scarcely curbed the ardor of a man so fresh from his preceptors and so tirelessly up-to-date. The two small nickel-plated tubs that Doctor Hodge was wont to use for sterilizing knives and saws in case of major operations only, appeared upon the scene and bubbled busily if any one so much as ran a sliver in his finger. The silver spoon that had held down tongues for countless throats went by the board; in its place appeared a tray of sanitary wooden spatulas. The friendly skeleton, so long a welcome guest at consultations, was banished to a cupboard shelf: "Of course you don't use it, do you, doctor?" the round-cheeked man had asked.

"It's just an outworn fetish, don't you think? Depresses people, when what they need is being cheered."

Even Simon Hodge's system of keeping books on scraps of wrapping-paper went into the discard. A file of index-cards supplanted it—so difficult to master that he found himself forever writing "street address" in "fever's" place, and "fever" in the little slot reserved for middle names.

There were intervals, in these adventures, when the old familiar office seemed a stretch of alien ground. Simon Hodge felt far from home. He couldn't get the index-cards in order, once he had them out. He couldn't knock his pipe against the office table; however old a magazine, the younger man insisted that an ashy flavor didn't help. He couldn't find his stethoscope; it was always being put in its right place again, instead of being left around.

At certain moments Doctor Hodge recalled the fact that this young man had been employed to bring him rest, and smiled a little wanly.

IV

There had been six months of innovation. Changes here and there, from time to time. A time-honored tumbler that had caught the water at the fountain since its first slow gurgle sat forlornly on a cupboard shelf, and saw its place usurped by little disks of paper. One evening Doctor Hodge came home and broke an unexpected bit of news. He was losing his assistant.

"Somebody in one of the city hospitals seems to have been keeping an eye on him. They 've offered him a job as interne."

"It 's a splendid chance!" said Simon's

wife. "Of course you won't stand in his way?"

"Oh, no. I can't do that."

"He's leaving right away?"

"Next week."

"But you 'll get some one else to take his place? Now, Simon, *promise* me. I won't have you getting tired."

"Well, of course I 'll have to see about it first. Can't move too fast, you know—and get a man who is n't up to scratch. Oh, yes, I suppose I 'll get somebody soon. Not right away, perhaps. May wait a little, first. These youngsters know their business, I suppose. I 'll tell you, Mary. Sometimes that fellow's nettled me a bit. You know. Changing things. But now that it comes to losing him, I 'll be fair enough to say that in lots of things I think he's right. You take those index-cards of his. Did I ever have a way of keeping

records till he came? No. I did n't. I 'll
admit it. And those cups. Confounded
nuisance, *I* say. Always folding up and
letting water down your sleeve. But sanitary, Mary. No doubt of that. Better
than that old chipped tumbler. And those
glass covers for the bandages. And that
skeleton. I dare say a man gets used to
things. Old friend of mine, that bony chap.
To tell the truth, I sort of miss him now.
Had him there so many years. But not
very cheerful, I suppose, if you happen to
be feeling blue. It takes these young fellows to come along and show us where we 're
wrong. We old-timers get in a rut, you
know. That boy has taught me lots of
things——"

He had sent the young man on his way
to the best luck in the world. Too late for
anybody in the office; but he 'd go back,

now, and get his satchel—then start home.

The gas-light sputtered in the waiting-room. Its pale tint lit the ceiling. In-direct lighting, the young man called it. Doctor Hodge preferred a friendly glare. Still, the young man was right, no doubt; this was easier on patients' eyes. Just one more of those new ideas to be written down. It takes the younger generation——

He crossed the room and tapped his pipe against the table. Hello! Better not do that. Flavor of ashes does n't help a mag-azine. As that young fellow used to say——

Used to say? . . . It is odd the way ideas dawn, sometimes. . . . Simon Hodge was tapping on the table now. Tapping with little even strokes that gathered vim. . . . Bright young lad, that fellow. Modern methods. Certain to go far. Already on his way. . . . He hit his pipe a sharp re-

sounding crack against the table. A
stream of ashes ran across the cover of his
newest journal. Nothing happened. Simon Hodge allowed himself a smile.

He opened the door of his consultation-
room and went inside. More lighting on
the ceiling here. The shade was made of
tin. He was surprised at the ease with
which it wrenched away. Ah! better now.
Good healthy glare.

A tower of small paper cups, sitting in
each other's haunches, caught his eye. He
threw them out of the window, watched
them strike the street below and roll. The
old glass tumbler was dusty when he sought
it on the cupboard shelf; but he wiped it
brazenly on a sanitary towel and let it wink
at him, with its bright nicks, when he thrust
it under the gurgling stream till it was full—
and drank.

The spoon. Where had that young man

hidden it? Well, the spoon could wait till morning. But there was time to lug the skeleton from its hiding-place and hang it on its iron hook. It was still swinging its lean legs in ecstasy when he turned out the lights and started home. The index-cards with their up-to-date accounting system made an inconvenient bundle for his arms. Still, it would be worth the effort. The office had a stove of course. But after all— for a merry blaze there's nothing like an open fire.

Sixty-six is well along in life to take on extra burdens. Doctor Hodge, as days went by, seemed to have no end of trouble filling his assistant's place. But his friends admitted he was plucky. Simon Hodge went on alone.

MRS. HENRY NESBIT

I

"THAT Nesbit woman! Wonder what
she's up to next?" There was a
time when Centerville discussed that question with a lively interest. But all that
ended one September morning. The town
heard Henry's Aunt Melissa was coming
home to stay.

Centerville, perhaps, had always been a
little jealous of Mrs. Henry Nesbit. Her
husband was the richest man in town. He
owned more stock than anybody else in the
interurban railway and the Merchants'
Bank, the Nesbit Dairy, and Consumer's
Coal & Ice. Mrs. Nesbit had an opulence
of leisure. She had no children. She had

no house to keep in order. Her servants
managed that. She had no worries with a
budget. In a community where the servant-
girl was a luxury shared only by the pros-
perous few, and the servant-girl herself had
usually the status of an adopted, if unlucky, daughter, Mrs. Nesbit employed a
cook, a laundress, and a well-trained maid.

What puzzled Centerville, in the affairs
of Mrs. Nesbit, was the rapidity with which
her interest shifted. There was that brief
era, for example—shortly after the end of
war in Europe—when Mrs. Nesbit took
up international politics. The magazines
were full of news, about that time, of
diplomats and new-born nations. Mrs.
Nesbit ordered from the city shops a shelf
of thirty books on world affairs, got up a
Study Club to debate the issues of a lasting
peace, and organized a pageant for relief
work that left her with a deficit of ninety

dollars. Her interest was devoted while it lasted. But the world moves on. Mrs. Nesbit, visiting Chicago with her husband, met a master in the art of auction bridge. The Study Club disintegrated gently when it got as far as freedom of the seas.

It was Mobray, known as an authority on doubled and redoubled bids wherever bridge is played, who put her through a series of six lessons. Centerville, in the weeks that followed, had those six reviewed. Home from her Chicago visit, Mrs. Nesbit rallied three recruits who had but lately struggled with the politics of Central Europe, and embarked upon a series of bridge afternoons: Mrs. Arthur Gregg, who would have read a . paper on "Aspects of the Reparations Tangle" if the Study Club had run another week; Mrs. Beard; and Mrs. Sallie Marshall. All the cunning of the Chicago master was impressed in turn upon these three. "My dear, you must *never* double when you have a chance of going game. Mobray says . . ."

Secretly, perhaps, the three recruits may have had enough of Mobray by the time the second rubber reached the books; may have wished, a little later, that the good man had never laid his eyes upon a knave of spades. It is not much fun to sit by silently and have each bit of one's own foresight ruled out as unconstitutional. Still, patience brought its own reward. These ladies had their innings later. Playing in other homes, less up-to-date than Mrs. Nesbit's, they stole that lady's thunder. "My dear, you must *never* double . . ."

Two camps sprang up in Centerville. But Mrs. Nesbit, about the time this controversy took a lively turn, lost interest in the great man altogether and swung around to Freud.

Psychology was what counted now. A new line of books adorned the parlor table. Mrs. Nesbit browsed a little, here and there. She did not always understand what she was reading, but that fact kept her interest up. Certain words and phrases she had made her own: "subconscious," "complex," "repression," and "libido." Her favorite was "complex." And there was little in the town to which she did not bring the interpretation of Repressed Desire.

Centerville discovered why Calvin Day so frequently forgot to take along his eartrumpet when he went to call upon his married sister, and little Millie Potter would n't eat the yellow of an egg.

II

It was at this juncture, to the consternation of Mrs. Nesbit's friends, and the pleas-

ure of her savage critics, that news of Aunt
Melissa's coming reached the town. No
more Freud, the critics said. No more
bridge. And no more freedom of the seas.
Aunt Melissa had the reputation of a tartar.

She had spent her life, this lady, under
the care of a self-sacrificing younger sister;
and now, having quarreled bitterly with
that faithful friend, for reasons undis-
covered, she turned for refuge to her
nephew. Henry seemed to think they
could n't turn her back. They had health
and money—she had neither. Centerville
remembered the old lady from two cyclonic
visits in the past. A woman well along toward sixty: imperious, quick-tempered, and
a finished egoist. For years she had been
a chronic invalid. She spent her days in a
wheel-chair, or propped against the pillows
of her bed. Her heart was subject to fits
of violent agitation. Her throat was del-

icate; she could n't stand the slightest draft. Sudden noises drove her to distraction. On occasion she had wept herself from grief to uncontrolled hysteria, because from some small oversight on the part of her exhausted sister she felt herself ignored.

She arrived, now, with chattels accumulated during the long period of her illness—smelling-salts and arm-chairs, medicines and worsted mufflers. Centerville had been wondering how Henry Nesbit's wife was going to take the news. Calmly, it seemed. She had the guest-room ready. She had moved the walnut bed across the hall, and put one in its place with shiny white enamel sides, and all the up-to-date devices of the hospital. She had put a sanitary chiffonier between one window and the fireplace: its rows of neatly ordered bottles bearing labels "Iodine" and "Alcohol" and "Calomel." She had ordered from the

city shops a chair with wheels that did most
things but start itself and climb the stairs.
She had installed a new gas heater and a
night alarm that rang a bell in case of sudden need. Aunt Melissa's illness had no
complication that could catch the household
unprepared.

It was remarkable, Mrs. Nesbit's friends
agreed, the way that lady met her husband's
aunt and took her to the bosom of the family. In the first two weeks of Aunt Melissa's stay she scarcely left the bedside.
Too busy, her friends found her, for the
Study Club that had been organized to
tackle Freud; too busy to spare time for
what the book-store purchased on approval.
Cynics said it would n't last; this was just
a bit of posing; Aunt Melissa would wake
up in that white enamel bed some day, and
find herself on a deserted island.

Certainly there was no more startled wit-

ness of this marked devotion than the invalid herself. For thirty years the chief
satisfaction Aunt Melissa had derived from
life was causing some one else a creditable
amount of trouble. It seemed to ease the
pain which she was sure she felt, at certain
times, to cry impatiently for water, when a
tumblerful sat on the table at her bedside.
There was no end of solace in complaining
—if some one left a window open in the
hall—that no one seemed to care a whit
what happened to a poor old woman, ready
for the grave. Best of all she liked to feel,
when it fell her lot to have a sleepless hour
before dawn, that one startled scream could
bring the household to her chamber.

Small satisfaction in these pleasures, if
you like; but all the satisfaction Aunt
Melissa had. And even of that little it
seemed in these first weeks of Centerville
that Fate intended to deprive her. A win-

dow open in the hall? Not once: not once
so much as half an inch. Henry's tireless
wife patrolled the hall—and had an extra
layer of weather-stripping put along the
panes. It had been so long since Aunt
Melissa had a chance to shiver slightly, draw
her worsted shawl around her throat, cough
twice, and look up wearily with patient eyes,
that there seemed a chance she might forget
the way to do it. As for turning out the
household at some hour well on the other
side of twelve and a good way short of six:
twice when Aunt Melissa raised her voice
this wife of Henry's had appeared so
promptly on the scene, so attractive in a
négligé that had been ordered from the city
for the very purpose—so unruffled in her
spirits and so willing to abandon thoughts
of her own bed, that Aunt Melissa gave it
up as scarcely worth the effort.

There were times in those first weeks, if

the truth be known, when one burnt bread-crust on a piece of toast would have been a godsend, and the soul of Henry's Aunt Melissa yearned for freedom like a long-imprisoned bird.

III

December brought the holidays. Aunt Melissa got no end of shawls and bed-pads from her nephew's wife. But Mrs. Nesbit made her stay in bed; it would n't do to risk excitement. Aunt Melissa could remember better holidays than that: holidays when she had sat in her sister's parlor and complained to Christmas guests that the smoke of burning candles made her head ache.

What was happening in the Nesbit household, neighbors could n't understand. At rare intervals her friends met Mrs. Nesbit on the streets. Had she lost her interest in the Study Club? Did she know that Mobray had reversed himself on doubling and not going game—and would n't she make a fourth at Mrs. Gregg's on Tuesday?

But Mrs. Nesbit only shook her head, to invitations of this sort, and said she could n't think of it. There was Aunt Melissa.

"You 'll forgive me, dear," she would explain; "I 'd love to come, but nowadays I have other things to keep me busy. That poor old soul just waits and waits for me. And then, you know, I 've started a little schedule now. It 's very interesting. There 's a little pad that hangs on the back of the door, and a pencil that goes with it. Just like the ones they have in the city hospitals—I had Henry bring it from Chicago. And every hour of the day there 's something to be done—like taking temperature, you know—and marking it with the pencil in a little square. It is n't very long. But

I wanted to be on the safe side, and so I added quite a lot of things. Aunt Melissa says it keeps her busy just being weighed and tested. But it's very interesting. And I'm sure it's helpful, too. Although she's a little more rebellious these days. I have to watch her all the time. She wants to get outdoors. Isn't it absurd, as sick as *she* is? Just pining for a little air, she says. Wants the windows open, but of course I can't have *that*. Even wants to leave her chair. Actually thinks that she could walk again—just fancy!—if I let her . . . Half-past four! My dear, I never guessed it was so late. I've been gone almost an hour. That poor soul is all alone. And then it's time to weigh her."

It was puzzling. For a woman who'd spent her life at fads, to settle down this way. . . . Mrs. Nesbit's critics couldn't understand it.

But Aunt Melissa could.

Mrs. Nesbit came home one afternoon, at the end of one of these infrequent lapses in her constant guard, and found a note propped on the mantelpiece. Aunt Melissa, content with what one suit-case carried, had gone back to her sister.

Gone back. And Malcolm Ross, whose shoe store fronts the railway-station, declares that when she came it was without assistance in the way of horse and cab—but on her own feet—and as if she were n't an invalid.

Moreover, Malcolm Ross avers that when he saw her she was running.

THE BROTHERS TEVIS

I

THERE was no love lost in the Tevis family. Except for one evening when it was too dark to recognize his brother on the street, and Dan had called out "Merry Christmas" to a man he thought a stranger, the two sons of Henry Tevis had n't spoken to each other once in twenty years.

The whole town knew about their quarrel. You can't split families in two, in a community of three thousand people, and not expect the neighbors to take sides. Centerville had its Guelphs and Ghibellines. Will's end of the block inclined toward Dan —Dan's end of the block inclined toward Will. But on the whole Dan seemed to have more friends behind him. Will, the town thought, was a little needlessly unbending in his ways.

He was the elder brother, Will: and from his father he had inherited a law practice and a way of rolling his eyes and tugging at his mustache when he talked. A man of fifty years: tall, slow-spoken, Will was meticulous in his care to say nothing without first giving the impression he had thought it over twice. Law practice in a small town is a forced march after clients. Will Tevis had n't prospered with the years. But he did n't forget that nowadays, as elder son, he flew the colors for the family: and Sunday afternoons he wore the frock-coat of his father with as much authority as its spare shoulders could command. "Second childhood," would be Dan's comment when his brother, thus arrayed, went past the parlor windows.

Dan was five years younger than his brother. He had the Tevis cheek-bones and the Tevis trick of rolling his eyes when he was reaching for a word that would n't come. But he was shorter than his brother, and more genial. In a way, he was the black sheep of the family. For he had declined to accept his father's counsel that he follow in the law, and tried, instead, a dozen different trades. At forty-five he had a business of his own. It paid him well. He built a larger house than Will's, with twice as many dormer-windows. No enterprise in town stood more firmly on its feet. But the business was n't law. "Used goods and curios," was the way Dan's wife described it. "Junk," was Will's more graphic phrase.

Three hundred feet apart, the Tevis houses—and yet so wide a gulf between that four intervening buildings might have been

a frontier. Nobody knew what had set
these brothers quarreling at the start.
Trouble dated back, some people thought,
to days when Will was big enough to pum-
mel Dan: and Dan, they said, was not the
sort who 'd ever have forgiven it. But that
was n't likely, other people pointed out; for
there had been interludes of friendship at
a later date than that. Ben Cole declared
these two had fought about their father's
will. But most people were inclined to
doubt it; the bones of the elder Tevis left
spare picking. Business rivalry was no ex-
cuse; there was no competition here. Nor
was it likely that Will aspired to unlawful
love of Mrs. Dan, and that Dan had found it
out, or vice versa; one look at either Mrs.
Tevis was proof enough of that. No one
was certain where the trouble lay. Even
the families had to guess at things.

"A Tevis in the junk trade! I would n't

trust him with a nickel," was as far as Mrs. Will had ever got.

"Stop pestering me about Will!" Dan would tell his wife. "You want to know 'What's the matter with him?' Do I have to tell you that? He makes me sick!"

Obscure enough in its causes, of this quarrel there was no mistaking the results. The whole block from Walnut Street to Maple felt its impact. If you were raking leaves and talking with Will, and caught with a corner of your eye a swift glimpse of Dan approaching farther up the street, you had either to send Will on his way with some remark so curt that it was likely to offend him, or else invent a garden-tool to search for, in the cellar, and leave both brothers to their fate. If you were a hostess with a party on your hands, you couldn't fill your table by inviting Mrs. Dan without offending Mrs. Will—or Mrs. Will without

affront to Mrs. Dan—or both without an im-
position on those fellow-guests who bore the
brunt of stony silence when the conversation lagged. For the Tevis women, as is
time-honored custom in fraternal wars, took
up the cudgels with the Tevis men. Even
the Tevis children, for all the light-handed-
ness of an impartial alphabet that sat them
side by side in school, had the fact impressed
on them at home that there must be no
fraternizing with the enemy. Millie Tevis
was whisked away to the State Fair, on
one occasion, to make up for her disappoint-
ment when she could n't go to dancing-
school; her cousin Bess had got there first.

To the children there was a good deal of
mystery in this family strife: and to the
neighborhood, for all the vicarious joy of
conflict, and the occasional satisfaction of a
choice of sides, it was something of a bore.
You could n't organize a business club or

send out invitations for a wedding supper without deciding first whether you would have the Dans or Wills included in the party. If Dan joined with his neighbors to petition for a paving bill, Will was sure to block the way and hold out for the status quo. When Will brought home a radio one night, Dan gave his son a sending set that cut in on ragtime from St. Louis with a disconcerting crackle. Centerville was ready to let the brothers Tevis choose their weapons for themselves. But there were times when everybody hoped that if they shot they 'd shoot to kill.

II

What could n't have been predicted was an accident to Will. He had been having his hair cut in Webster's basement barber shop, one afternoon, and toppled over with a

stroke when he had climbed the steps. It
did n't cripple him; he was back in court
within four weeks. But the unexpectedness
of what had happened opened things afresh.
It was time, the whole town felt, to go back
and begin again.

Nobody knows, now, whether it was a
peace-loving neighborhood or members of
the family circle who first began negotia-
tions. But to Will the point was strongly
stressed that one stroke often follows on
another's heels, and that Dan was just the
sort who 'd do his best to make things hard
for Bess and Eddie when no father stood
on guard, unless some sort of peace were
patched up in good season. Meantime Mrs.
Dan suggested to her husband, and all the
Caldwells and the Davidsons agreed, that
there was just enough sheer spite in Will
to drag his brother through the public prints
with some outrageous passage in a widely

published will, too late for any answer. Optimistic friends on both sides had gone further. Old Henry Tevis, they suggested, must be broken-hearted in his grave. Why not seize this happy chance to clear things up—effect an old-time understanding? Grudgingly, on his sick-bed, Will Tevis had agreed to hold his temper if his brother came to offer peace. As for Dan: in the end it seemed the better part of valor to give way, lest in his own good health he seem unsportsmanlike in having had no stroke to match his brother's. They would meet—and have it out alone. Dan had suggested that the room be cleared of its unnecessary women.

It seemed to mark a turning-point in Tevis history, that April afternoon when flags of truce appeared on Market Street, and a short man well out of breath toiled up forgotten steps to greet a lean and tired brother. In the hall outside Will's door, and on a porch three hundred feet away, two families watched the clock uneasily and waited for the issue.   The room was barred. But eager minds could see the picture: Will, wan and earnest on his bed—Dan ill at ease beside him, tracing with one toe the pattern in a Brussels carpet.   There would come a question first.   Then Will, or maybe Dan, would plunge straight to the heart of things. What had been festering for twenty years —what, from the distant first, had been the cause of this unfathomable quarrel—would come out like a thorn drawn slowly from a wounded foot.   Points of view obscure for many years would be explained; misunderstandings brushed away like bread-crumbs from a table.   Either that—or hot words, and a quarrel worse than ever.

Will faced his brother in the sick-room. And what happened, no one in the hall, or

on the porch, would have been quite ready
to imagine.

Dan was the first to speak. "Tough
luck," he said—he was standing at the foot
of the bed, and fumbling with the cover.
"Sort of caught you unexpected, did n't it?"

Will grunted. "It's those damned
steps," he said. "Steep enough to make
anybody's heart go like a whistle. I'll
never have my hair cut in that place again."

Dan nodded. "That's the trouble with
a basement shop. I'd go to Frye's if I was
you."

"Frye's all right," acknowledged Will.
"Webster's a better barber, though."

"Oh, I ain't so sure of that," suggested
Dan. "Frye's just as good. In fact, I
dare say better."

"Better nothing!" Will had his own con-
victions on that point. "I've been having

my hair cut in Webster's place for twenty
years——"

"All right, all right," agreed his brother.
"Your hair 's not all the hair in town."

"Don't you tell me who 's the better barber," Will said warmly. "I 'm not asking
your advice."

"You would n't get it if you did," responded Dan. "Anybody 'd be a fool to
waste the effort. As long as I remember,
you 've been just that stubborn."

"Stubborn? Don't call *me* stubborn!"
shouted Will, so firmly that the listeners in
the hall thought, Ah! the secret 's out. "I
won't take any talk from your sort!" Will
hitched himself across the pillow, with a mut-
tered "Junk!"

Dan walked to the window, looked out on
Market Street, then chose a chair and
dragged it to the bedside. For a time he sat

there quietly, observing with interest the ice-bags on his brother's head.

Will broke the silence. "The Missis was telling me—" he said.

"I know," said Dan. "If you 're agreeable, I suppose we might as well."

Will nodded. Dan kept rocking. It was n't for five minutes that he rose to go. "We 're friends again, then, Will?"

"As long as it 's *you* that asked for it," said Will.

Dan opened the door. "All right."

Fresh earth lay on the Tevis hatchet.

III

News of a reconciliation spread swiftly through the town, and for the moment held its interest. Mrs. Dan stopped Mrs. Will on Market Street, and in full view of half a dozen neighbors kissed her on both cheeks. Mrs. Will invited Mrs. Dan to join her study club. Mrs. Dan entertained at bridge, and in a tuft of tissue-paper bestowed a guest-of-honor token on her sister. Young Ned Tevis found a new third baseman for his baseball team. Millie Tevis hurried into dancing-school and traded secrets with her cousin Bess. Neighbors up and down the street congratulated one another on the dawn of peace: yet felt, somehow, that there had been a let-down. Was it over, after all these years, with no more fireworks than that? And was n't anybody going to learn the secret? Fred Wiles, who lived next door to Dan, averred he had it on the best authority that there had been a woman in the case. Will had forbidden Dan to have anything to do with her, or Dan had accused Will of stowing her away, or something of the sort. In the whole affair the least display of interest was manifested by the brothers Tevis.

Dan had called on Will a second time, while he was still confined indoors. Will had responded by lending Dan an album which he had no desire to carry up the street. It was tacitly agreed that they would speak cordially when they met in public, and withdraw blackballs against each other in two lodges neither wished to join. But the bargain left them uninspired. Something that belonged securely in the center of their lives seemed worn away, and the unacknowledged problem was discovering what it was. Dan, whose even temper was n't often ruffled, began to sulk a little with his family. Will declared he doubted if he 'd ever be himself again, and talked about "old times." To ask either brother how he felt about the aftermath of this new peace was to court an answer unpredicted in its sharpness.

Mrs. Dan might trump her sister's clubs and diamonds in the flutter of an unexpected intimacy; but the male Tevises chose to weather out this peace alone.

A fortnight passed. Will was on the street again. The moodiness of the two brothers had deepened measurably. Dan had quarreled with his daughter Millie because he promised her a dress. Will would push his chair back from the table, with his plate filled, and declare he "was n't hungry." One evening, on the curbstone, fortune gave the Tevis wheel another twist.

It was the first time these two had faced each other on the street, away from the confining presence of a sick-room. Dan had left his house and started for the corner store, and a cigar. It had been his practice, for twenty years, to march along on his own side of the street until he came to the edge of his brother's property: then cross the street as ostentatiously as possible, to impress the members of his brother's household with the fact no berth could be too wide for them. He was half-way across the street from sheer force of habit now, when with a pang of ill-defined regret the thought came home to him that no longer was there any reason for this wide detour. He swung back, it happened, precisely at the moment when his brother Will, whose own part in this time-honored pantomime required that he now be standing with his back turned to the street, to indicate to Dan how little all this troubled him, chose also to remember that the feud was at an end, and turned to meet his brother. Silent, ill at ease, they faced each other: caught red-handed in the act.

Slowly Dan came back across the gravel roadway till he reached the curb. Old Mrs. Dyke, toiling up the far side of the street with a market-basket on her arm, would have let it drop and hurried to the scene of action had she dared.

"I 'm not afraid of you, Dan Tevis," Will shouted from the sidewalk, "if that 's what you mean by spinning around there, in the middle of the street, as if you meant to have a fling at me."

"Don't stand there and preach at me!" retorted Dan. "I guess I can walk on your sidewalk if I want to."

"You can walk on the sidewalk," Will replied, as if he 'd thought it over many times. "But if you step on my grass I 'll have the law on you."

"You will, eh? There! I 've stepped on your grass. What are you going to do about it?"

"Get off my lawn!"

"You come and put me off."

"That 's enough, Dan Tevis! I take

back what I said about forgetting."

"You do, eh? If you think——"

"Your family, too! I don't want my Missis hobnobbing with your wife."

"You could n't get my wife to look at her. I 'll tell her about this. Here! Let go, now. Let go my coat-lapel. Take your hands off, Will Tevis, or by cracky! I 'll—"

Two hours later, when Dan Tevis had told his wife that the truce was at an end, and Will Tevis had gathered his family around him to explain that Dan had gratuitously insulted him within ten feet of his own porch, twilight had fallen over Centerville. Dan Tevis had his daughter on his knee, hunting through a catalogue of dresses. Will Tevis had eaten his first real supper in four weeks, and sent his wife to the pantry for more pie.

It would be war to-morrow. All Market

Street would hear the trumpet-call. But to-night a strange peace had settled on the brothers Tevis.

Something lost had come back home again.

MADAME NALDA

I

FROM the soiled pack resting in a ruddy palm, Madame Nalda dealt the cards. Many things the queens and treys and six-spots told her. One they did n't. That happened to be the one for which she cared.

There is a boarding-house or two in every town where refugees from the wrecks of early hopes find shelter. It is a patchwork building in a quiet street, pervaded by an air of decent ruin. The doors have lost their shutters; the walls are shedding paint. One basement window holds aloft an open palm, and bids the passer-by descend into a world whose tense is manifestly past, to read the message of the future.

In Centerville this basement lodging had a steady boarder. You could catch a glimpse, behind a window-box of pale geraniums, of a bulky woman wrapped in printed cotton challie who sat beside a window, sewing, while she overflowed a rocking-chair. It was twenty years, at any rate, the town would tell you, since Madame Nalda came to Centerville. Well past forty, she was then—and very much a widow in her weeds. She had a boy with her in those days: a silent youngster in his early teens. Nobody in the boarding-house could remember what had happened to the boy; but Madame Nalda had been sewing at the window ever since she found this basement home. Alone, and on its own score, fortune-telling never paid its way.

Interest lagged; it may be there is a

skepticism in the younger generation alien
to the old days. Certainly Madame Nalda
often went six days on end without so much
as dusting off the crystal ball to catch a
glimpse of the hereafter. There were a few
faithful friends who came for consultation
when they lost their keys or lacked the last
decisive ounce of valor for a business deal.
But for the most part Madame Nalda's
patrons now were youngsters on a lark.
They came in pairs; they took the whole
performance lightly. Three aces in a row
conveyed no terror to the young. They
winked at warnings, laughed at fate.

How much of her own story Madame
Nalda trusted, as she turned the cards, not
even the crystal ball could tell you. Very
little in the old days. She felt a vague
foreboding then of something good or bad
to happen, as each new client came her way.
She played on that. She watched for open-

ings, and made her guest disclose his worries when he talked. She trusted luck. But she would never have claimed, to a protesting conscience, that she saw behind the veil. These people wanted to be entertained; fifty cents was a pledge of faith; what right had she to thwart them?

That was in the old days. To guess the truth was not so easy now. Madame Nalda mumbled a little when she sewed; there were gaps of silence when she dealt the cards. She felt that she was talking with some spirit restless in its disembodied home. And this time the crystal ball could give a clear-cut answer. The trouble was the boy.

II

He was a youth of fourteen when he came to Centerville: a pale lad with startled eyes and a certain murkiness of spirit which Madame Nalda declared the gift of his departed father. She was proud of him, and used to boast to the guests assembled overhead for supper that he never gave her any trouble. "He's quick as lightning with his lessons," she would say. "I know he must be. He's in the high school now, and how many times do you think his teachers have come and said he wasn't doing right? Just once. Oh, he's a smart one."

He had kept his father's name, the boy: not Nalda, but the more prosaic Nelson. Now and then, if you had been in Centerville when this odd couple came to town, you might have seen him trailing the curb behind his mother when she swept through Market Street. That, most likely, would be some day when keys enough had been discovered, and happy endings prophesied for happy lovers, to furnish funds for a shopping tour. The boy objected to these trips.

He was old enough, he said, to choose the clothes he wanted for himself. His mother disabused him. There were traders, she affirmed, whose special joy it was to pounce on boys his age and sell them caps that warp and underclothes that shrivel. Nothing of this sort could happen with a watchful mother. And so they made a pair: the mother striding on ahead—a giant woman, capable, if fortunes could be told that way, of wresting secrets from the heart of destiny by force of arms—halting on the way sometimes to ask the boy a question: was he tired? did he see the hook-and-ladder when they passed the fire-station? had his teacher ever told him what they call those trees with furry branches? The boy himself, meantime, a pace or two behind her—scowling, silent—swept on against his will, by lack of weight: a piece of driftwood in the wake of some sea-going liner.

So seldom did these two appear upon the streets together that not many people in the town identified young Nelson with the crystal-gazing of his mother. Perhaps it was some such discovery as that, on the part of his young friends in school, that led the boy to drop his classes early in his stay in Centerville. He had a morbid fear of being laughed at—that, too, his mother said, he had acquired from his father—and the chances are his friends had teased him when they learned about his mother's trade. He said nothing on that score; but announced one night that he had had enough of school and planned to start in running errands for the grocery. His mother stormed at that. Who was he, to throw away his chances? She had meant to see that he went on from school to college. Boys had been known to work their way before. She would help him as she could; he could depend on that.   He would come back here some day prepared to take his teacher's place.   They would see who laughed last in this wretched boarding-house.   Those people at the supper-table, with their taunts at spooks and fortune-telling—let them wait! What would they say when this boy of hers was miles beyond them—in the high school, teaching something hard, like algebra or Latin?

In the end the boy won out.   It must have been a heartless gibe his comrades threw at him.   And having lost the struggle, Madame Nalda made a virtue of defeat.   This boy of hers, she told the supper-table, was not the sort who'd be content to loaf his way through school.   He was a born worker —like his father.   Did she have to tell him, now, that the time had come to make a start? Not likely.   Her boy was not the kind who needed prompting of that sort.   He had

come to her and told her that the grocery
had been urging him to take a job. And a
very wise decision he had made. There was
a future in a trade like that. He meant to
learn the business from the bottom.

In her own imagination Madame Nalda
sheltered even finer visions. The boy would
study law as he grew older, and began to
have a clearer sense of what was right and
what was wrong. You could hold a job and
learn to be a lawyer in the evenings. She
had heard of many men who did it just that
way. Of course you needed books. Her eyes
were strong; they were n't half tired with
her sewing; she would see he had the books
he wanted. And law was even better than
school-teaching. There were fees a man
could earn: huge fees with which you
bought a house and raised a family. Law-
yers could be judges. Her son would be
a credit to his trade. People would point

him out as a man who'd made his way un-
aided. He would marry some day. No
daughter of the Gipsies. A girl whose family had solid prestige in the town. They
would have a house on Chestnut Street with
a fountain in the yard.

Madame Nalda dreamed of great things
coming. She read a happy future in the
cards.

III

Whatever his virtues, young Nelson's
forte had never been his conversation. He
was a moody lad. On rare occasions you
could hear him whistling when he left the
house. Madame Nalda would part the geraniums in a hurry when that happened, and
lean across the window-sill to watch him
down the street. Whistling. She would
smile and shake her head. Like his father.

But a time came when the whistling stopped, and the boy's silence settled down on him. He would leave his mother in the evening with a hazy story of his plans. They would sit at supper—that was an affair no longer shared above-decks with the boarders; times were hard, and the revenue from fortune-telling meager; Madame Nalda found that she could save by cooking on a gas-jet—and sometimes it took coaxing to win so much as yes or no from the thin lips of this somber boy.

It was engineering now. Madame Nalda had lost none of her enthusiasm with the years. Those pamphlets; had he looked at them? An hour's study in the evening. That was what they said; no more. An hour. Some of the greatest engineers in the country——

Did n't he remember how much electric things had interested him when he was a

boy? There was that train his father gave
him one time for his birthday. Did n't he
remember—with the yellow roof? That
boy next door had wound it up too tight.
Nobody had a better chance these days than
people in electric things. You could make
a fortune if you hit it right. You could be
looked up to by your neighbors. You
could own a house in the best part of town.
A big house with a garden.

The boy would hear her out in silence.
He was a young fellow, now, of twenty-two.
It was eight years since he had started at the
bottom of his grocery. He had left that
soon; even, in fact, before his mother had decided, on the best of evidence, that there were
others things for which her son was better
fitted than the law. She had gone on then
to banking, architecture, medicine: while the
boy, meantimes, had gravitated from the
grocery to a foundry, and the foundry to a

clothing store. He was doing well enough to-day. He had come to rest behind the counter in the freight-depot of the railway, earning for himself a living wage. Madame Nalda used to pride herself on his frugality. He did n't spend his earnings in the streets, and did n't bring them home. He gave his money to a bank.

Putting by his savings for a house in Chestnut Street?

No. He had a better plan than that.

IV

Her name was Madge. He 'd met her in a picture-show. There 'd never been a girl like this before.

Pretty? Blue eyes and yellow hair; wore her clothes like pictures in the Sunday papers; sometimes when they went into Malley's candy store the whole room turned to

look at her. He 'd had a battle on his
hands. If he had n't promised to take her
out of Centerville, he might have lost her
more than once. She did n't like the town.
The city was the place for her, she said;
they 'd go, he promised, when he found a
job. Could n't his people help him? she
would ask.

He was a little vague about his people.
There was a reason why. One time, very
early in their story, on a Sunday's walk
they 'd passed a boarding-house. It was
late afternoon. They were on the other
side. But the girl had seen a sign
across the street. An open palm; an
invitation to the passer-by to have his
fortune told. "Let 's go!" she had suggested.

He shook his head. He 'd rather not, he
said.

"Oh, come. We 'd have some fun."

"Do you think you'd find out anything you don't know now?"

"Of course not, silly. We wouldn't go for that. We'd go to have a laugh."

She started for the curb, but he took her arm and pulled her back.

"Come on!" she said. "Let's see what this one's like. They're great, sometimes."

He didn't want to go, he said again. And how was she to tell about it anyway? This woman might be different.

"Different? Sure she's different. That's why I want to go. They're queer ones, *they* are. Of course they're funny, most times. But spooks—and all that. It's just like traveling with a side-show. You know. Freaks."

She tugged at his arm, but he was stubborn. He told her that his head ached. Not now, he pleaded. Too nice a day outdoors; they'd go some other time.

"Outdoors!" she jeered. "You're always talking of outdoors. I suppose because it doesn't cost you anything. Oh, you're all right. I know you're saving money so's we can blow this town. But say, you never do a thing I want to do. When I say, 'Let's us go and dance'—*you* say, 'Oh, I'd rather walk around the Public Square.' Well, that's all right. I ain't objecting. But we can't stand and feed the goldfish *all* the time."

They compromised on going to a movie.

Madame Nalda used to wonder what her son did evenings. Office-work, he hinted sometimes. She told him that was right; night-work was everything; it sent a young man on.

He was doing well, she told herself. Of course this wasn't law or engineering. The boy hadn't really started his career. Still, railroading itself might prove to be the thing. There were great executives, she read, who got their first instruction in the yards.

There was time ahead; the boy was laying a foundation now. What troubled her was the way this silence gripped him. Was he tired? Had he worked too hard? Another job might give him time for rest—and study. If she could add an hour's sewing to the day . . . One evening all that ended. Madame Nalda spent her whole life telling fortunes.

But the boy just disappeared.

CAPTAIN FOLEY

I

FAR and away the brightest spot on Market Street, after nine o'clock, was Elmer Bradley's billiard parlor. When the rest of the block from the interurban station to the Baptist Church had gone to bed, there would always be two friendly arc-lights cutting disks of creamy white on Mr. Bradley's sidewalk. Long after the last postage-stamp of the evening had found its way across the counter in Martin's corner drug store, the red door of Mr. Bradley's parlor still swung to the shoves of genial billiardists. From the street you heard the click of ivory on ivory; the faint distant thud of a weary ball that had dropped to its appointed pocket.

It was home, this place, for a patron well along in middle age whose hours life had spaced between good humor and romance. Geniality radiated from a ruddy face, from two wide-parted eyes and a broad smile with a clink of metal in it, like the grimace of a tea-pot when you lift the cover with your thumb. Captain Foley was as gay as any troubador who lived for a guitar. A gentleman of leisure from sunrise till late afternoon, inasmuch as play was seldom started in the pool-room until four o'clock.

It was n't always pool, of course. There were days when Captain Foley turned his hand to unproductive labor. That would be at times when a brother turned him out of a congenial home—and the Captain earned his daily bread by pruning trees or pasting bills until he 'd worked himself into the good graces of a married sister. The pool-room missed him in these interruptions of his leisure hours. But the interruptions never lasted long. Captain Foley had no end of brothers, sisters, cousins, whose friendliness he could capture at decisive moments. And once a door had opened wide enough to let him get a foot inside, he dropped whatever tool the peril of starvation had put between his hands, and turned in triumph to the bright arc-lights of Elmer Bradley's pool-room.

Never a customer who added more distinction to the place. The red door of Mr. Bradley's parlor would bang upon its hinges. "Gentlemen, I bid you one and all good afternoon!" Captain Foley would be back again. He would hook his coat on the short-armed rack that grew in the marshy floor behind the water-cooler, and advance, with an exchange of friendly insults as he passed each group of players, to the choosing of an ash.

Four rows of cues adorned the walls. One row had no tips. A second row had tips but also locks—aristocrats, here, of the cue world—as individual, as sanitary, and as little used as the gold-initialed shaving-mugs on the top shelf in Webster's barber shop. Two racks left; from one of them the Captain chose his lance. "Open break, or closed?" he asked his adversary.

If closed, the gentle bumping of the corner ball against a once resilient cushion.

If open, then the fury of the whirlwind in his forward thrust; a lunge that would drive a saber through a safe door.

Nobody put more spirit into Elmer Bradley's ritual than this patron whose swift shots were all too often made on credit.

II

There was a long hall, in Bradley's place, with six great bandy-legged tables straddling it. Their green tops sparkled in the glare of drop-lights: water-holes with sharp reflections in a dark Sahara. The long cords that held the bright bulbs swayed; the whole room rocked in light and shadow. Black patches chased each other up the walls, chased each other down again. You caught swift glimpses of champions who looked down from tessellated picture-frames: Dan Patch, who paced the mile in one fifty-seven and a quarter; Cy Young, with one stout arm whipped back to send his cannon-ball across the plate; Ad Wolgast, a hundred and thirty-three pounds ring-side, trained to the pink of condition and girdled with a flag.

More than once, when the lights were n't

swinging high enough to throw a glare on the picture-frames, these masters had looked down on Captain Foley's triumphs. All manner of variations in the way he played his shots: the resounding boom of a fugitive, cornered after two escapes and fairly blasted; the high-arched thumb and nervous stab that made the simplest shot look difficult; the "back spin," theoretically imparted at the bottom of the ball, that took up an inch or two of speed and occasionally an inch of table. Captain Foley often had a crowd around his table. He would chalk his cue with nonchalance, and study the next shot warily while the gallery discussed what would have happened to the last one had he played it differently. And all the time, if his was the new table from Chicago equipped with subterranean passageways, the dead balls coursed with a satisfactory hollow rattle along the corridors of time, to drop like striped and numbered Easter eggs into a wicker basket.

III

Long shots were all right in their way; but Captain Foley's prestige rested on more solid ground. There were times when the whole room stopped its play to pack itself in chairs around the water-cooler, and listen to his stories. Captain Foley plumbed the seven seas.

How any man could have packed so much within a span of years so short was something of a puzzle. It was true that the Captain had run away when he was still a youngster; that he had shipped before the mast and later spent a winter logging in the West and traveled for a season with a circus. But he had been back home for many years by this time; his wild oats fell between the ages of sixteen and twenty. That left a margin of five years. But five would scarcely do, if one stood with a billiard-cue and counted off time's passage on the wooden markers over Bradley's tables. Certainly, to listen to these stories, there had been at least three years at sea—two years on the China coast—two more in Mexico; three seasons with the circus—a winter spent in Spain; and that was taking no account of a journey through the Malay woods, a single-handed tussle with the Colorado Cañon in a well nigh foundering canoe, and that vague association with the army which had won the title "Captain." Fred Hovey figured out one time, on the cover of a box of billiard-balls, that if half of what had happened to this man were reckoned true, he must have run away at four and come back home at sixty.

In any case, one thing was true. Nothing happened nowadays that had not figured in this soldier's past. A tornado in the Philippines? So the city paper said. "I can well believe it," would be Captain Foley's comment as he chalked his cue. "One time—I was sailing in a clipper then —we were heading for Manila when we struck a gale——"

That was n't all. So keen was Foley for a life of romance at first hand that adventure still pursued him through the quiet streets of Centerville. "You know that sign above Jim Martin's store—the one that crashed down in the storm this afternoon? Well, sir, let me tell you that I just happened to be going by the very minute it came down—and it did n't miss my head by half a foot. Would have knocked me flatter than a pancake!"

No other life in Centerville hung by so slim a thread. Captain Foley's was a never-

ending series of flirtations with some sudden
death. Live wires lashing in the streets,
and dogs that might have bitten and were
surely mad; a box of pellets on a cupboard
shelf, where his sister Emma always kept
her cough-drops—turning out, the very moment he had put one tablet on his tongue,
to be a preparation guaranteed to rid the
house of rats.

No one in Bradley's parlor thought that
Captain Foley's tales were true. But all of
Bradley's patrons let their cues fall when a
story started, and came flocking to the
scene.

There was one tale, dating back to circus
days, that Foley chose on state occasions.

He was chief trainer in those days.
Duke, biggest of the elephants, had broken
loose. It was in the little town of Freeport, Tennessee. Duke headed for the
wilds, but tumbled in a river. Captain

Foley, with a clump of hay tied to his back above the water-line, had swum against the current—to lead the puzzled Duke to shore again.

That story always brought a chorus of loud hoots. "Go on now, Cap!"— "Say, who ever told you that one?"— "Cap, you ought to have a year in jail!"

Billiardists went back to frozen cue-balls, chuckling. But Captain Foley held his ground.

"Fact," he'd say. "Right in the center of the little town of Freeport. I could take you to the very spot to-day."

IV

The string of markers on the wires overhead would never have been long enough to count the times that story had been told— the jeers it had received. But one night

the rescue of the errant Duke encountered
something new. No hoots, this time.
Fate sent a witness to the scene.

It was a Saturday night, and Bradley's
parlor did a rushing business. All three
tables had been clicking steadily since
supper-time. Two traveling salesmen had
the front one: lean men, idling an hour from
the clock before they called it time for bed.
From behind the water-cooler the story of
the river rescue was unfolding for the bene-
fit of three new friends. The clump of hay
was tied in place—the Captain half-way
down the slippery bank. "There he stood,
that old tusker, in the middle of the river,
splashing water with his trunk and trumpet-
ing his fool head off. I struck out for the
other shore——"

From the table underneath the bright
electric bulbs a traveling salesman edged
his way across the room.

"I beg your pardon, brother," he began, "but I could n't help over-hearing what you said. Where did you say this happened?"

Play stopped, at all of Mr. Bradley's tables. Sensing a new dénouement for the rescue scene, the whole room crowded up to listen.

Captain Foley turned to face his questioner.

"Why, in Freeport," he declared. "The little town of Freeport, Tennessee. Perhaps you did n't hear the story from the start. If you don't mind"—this to the three friends beside the water-cooler—"I 'll just begin again."

"I heard it from the start," the traveling salesman said, "and I came over here to ask a question because Freeport, Tennessee, happens to be my town."

"Yes?" Captain Foley was all interest.

"I don't know what you 're trying to put over, neighbor," the man from Freeport said, "but don't you know that no elephant could have jumped into a river? There is n't any river in that town."

"No river? Why, I tell you——"

"No river," the traveling salesman said, "and no creek. Not a puddle. That town 's famous, friend. Driest place in Tennessee. Why, except for wells you have to drive six miles for water enough to wash your face. Maybe your elephant was sitting in a wash-tub."

There are moments when the bottom drops from a story so completely that it brings a thud. There are also moments when an alien volunteers advice that no one 's asked for.

Captain Foley rose beside the water-cooler. "Gentlemen," he said, in a voice

that carried dignity to ranks of Mr. Bradley's guests.   "I ask you if I have not told
that story here before?"

"Yes!"   Walls echoed with the shout.

"I ask you if anybody has ever cast the
slightest doubt on it before—so much as
hinted it was not God's truth?"

"No!"

"I ask you, finally, whether anything this
gentleman says has shaken confidence in
me?"

"No!"

"Thank you, gentlemen."

With a wave of his hand, Captain Foley
found his chair again.   "As I was saying,
I struck out for the other shore——"

The stranger shrugged his shoulders;
went back to his game.

Night wore on.   Smoke banked itself in
layers on Mr. Bradley's ceiling.   One by
one the green pools of light winked out in

darkness. The red door swung to the shoves of uncrowned champions. "Good night Eddie. Don't take any wooden money."

Still the talk went on. Captain Foley, having had his good faith questioned, was driving home the doubtful point. It was a new tale on which he 'd started now. Another Freeport story.

This time the famous flood.

LUCY WALLIS

SOME people stumble into romance, and other people chart the countryside and try to run it down. Take Lucy Wallis, for example, and the young man with the eye-shade.

Lucy Wallis had been dedicated to some useful, cultivated labor from the start; her family had done its best to see that she would never go to seed or lose herself in easy pleasure. She had gone without a hitch through school and college; kept on afterward, from the force of her momentum, to win herself a graduate degree. She talked of doing social work, of teaching school, of going out to some warm Eastern land to help the church spread gospel. In the end she chose to stay with books, went back to school again, and finished one last course of training as a librarian. It was pure chance that when it came her turn to find an opening, the Fates decreed her Centerville.

Not for long, before this opportunity arrived, had books in Centerville possessed a home that they could call their own. For years "the library" had been a room above a shoe store: so closely guarded on one flank by the Scylla of a moving-picture show, and on the other by Charybdis in the guise of Malley's combination candy and cigar store, that only the most determined seekers after book-lore found the straight and narrow path between. The scene had shifted by the time the new librarian arrived. Thanks to the last will and testament of Henry Nesbit, Sr., the literary heritage of Centerville had come to rest in a low-roofed mausoleum of its own.

Lucy Wallis found a place to live, around the corner from this job of hers, boarding with a family of pioneers. She came to work at nine o'clock, and stayed at night until eight thirty. At noon and suppertime she had an alternate to take her place. The rest of the day the four-room building was her own. There was a reading-room—with a file of index-cards and two racks of magazines hung up like chickens in a market by their necks; a stack-room—cases of non-fiction backed against the farther wall, at bay before advancing hordes of romance; a "children's room," so called, Lucy Wallis was ready to decide, at the end of her first week of work, because occasionally the children ran through it when they used the halls for tag.

This was all, down-stairs; three rooms

closely crowded. But overhead, reserved
for special Sundays in the winter months,
and then thrown open for the afternoon, the
attic sheltered a Museum. Portraits, here,
of Henry Nesbit—of George Loring, the
town's first mayor—of Matthew Kent, who
came back from the Cuban war a major.
Authentic bits of early Centerville displayed in glass-topped cases: a chart of the
town in '43, a deed of land for its first
school, a draft-list from the days of Chicka-
mauga. Here and there a gift less highly
prized, but difficult to spurn without offense
to kindly giver: an arrow-head, a stone run
down and trampled by the glaciers, a cro-
chet portrait of McKinley, a lump of lava
from Mount Etna.

Which one of these four rooms most
closely touched the lives of people in the
town, Lucy Wallis was n't certain. The
stack-room pumped a steady flood of fiction

through perhaps three hundred homes. The Museum had its special friends, who came to see what comments their own gifts brought forth. The children's room had possibilities.

But tact alone would not make Mother Goose and Lives of Great Inventors as popular as hunting through the picture-books and tearing out the lions.

II

Time, meanwhile, had kept the promises it made when Lucy Wallis was a child. In these days of Centerville there was nothing of the elf about her; no foibles and no shams. She was as plain and manifestly to be trusted, and if the truth be told as un-compelling to the eye, as when, a little girl of four, her parents brought her in before the guests assembled in the parlor.

She was about thirty now; a tall girl with ruddy hair that might have carried off successfully some gayer bangle than the 2B pencil she would stick above her ear when she was cataloguing books. Her skin was smooth and softly colored; but only an indulgent uncle, years ago, had called her handsome. Her cheeks were thin; her lips were pale; her eyes were handicapped by thick round lenses that struggled with astigmatism. She had been taught, as a child, that bright colors did not go with red hair and a sense of duty. Her dresses were a serviceable gray.

Not that it made much difference, in the run of things, what clothes she wore: provided they were warm enough or cool enough, and not so dark or light that they would show the dust that covered Burke and Boswell's Johnson. She did n't know the sort of people here who entertained at par-

ties. She did n't easily make friends. Of
those she had, the most familiar was a
woman with a shawl who came to read a
paper from Chicago. She used to live
there, she explained, and liked to read the
ads and see what bargains she 'd have had
if she had stayed. Another regular was a
veteran of '61 who brought his own book
with him when he came, and read it in a
corner. There was a school-boy launched
on Kipling, and a girl who copied first-aid
data from the magazines. And then there
was the young man with the eye-shade.

Lucy Wallis had found out what there
was to know of him before he came the second time. "Professor" was his title in the
town. Like herself, he was a stranger here.
He was teaching mathematics in the high
school: a young man—sandy-haired, square-
faced, immensely serious. He would bring
a leather brief-case with him, and sometimes

spread its contents on a table in the reading-room and start correcting papers. Lucy Wallis decided he was quite as lonely in his boarding-house as she felt in her own.

He would come in quietly, close the door as softly as though this were a sick-room, put his bag down on a table, hang his hat behind the door, and disappear into the stack-room. Usually it took him quite a time to find the book he wanted. Then he would come back across the reading-room again, this time on tiptoe, and, because his shoes creaked, not so quietly. He would choose a chair as near a light as he could get and hook an eye-shade on his ears. From that time forth there was no disturbing him until the hour came to dim the lights.

Lucy Wallis never knew what book this silent man was reading. He always put it back in its right stall before he left the building. She used to watch, when he was working, to see if he would steal a glance her way. She never caught him doing it, and never drew from him a more responsive greeting than a nod. She was sorry that was so. He was a student. He was lonely. There was a good deal they might have talked about, a good many interests they might share. More interests than she had in common with the Chicago lady or the people in her boarding-house or the high-school boys who came to her in search of topics for their essays.

It was a little dreary in the evenings after half-past eight. Lucy Wallis was well schooled in the indifference of men. They had been hanging their hats behind the door and nodding their good evenings from across the room for fifteen years. But here was a lost waif like herself. Friendship, and a break in the routine of empty eve-

nings: surely that much lay within the
bounds of reason.

III

There was always an even chance that the
reading-room would be deserted after seven
forty-five, and to-night the place was quiet.
Lucy Wallis and the young man with the
eye-shade had it to themselves. A clock
above the rack of papers raked the room
with even ticks. The young man was reading; he had been sitting there since half-
past six, elbows on the table, eyes intent
upon the slowly turning pages underneath
the light.

Lucy Wallis had a book she liked; but
she had watched this man uneasily for half
an hour. And now she slid the top drawer
of her desk half open, let the book slip into
it, and walked across the room.

"I 'm sorry to disturb you—" she began.

The young man rose, unhooked his eye-shade from his ears, and peered at her through glasses quite as prepossessing as her own.

"A new book came to-day," she said. "I thought I 'd speak to you about it. You might want to read it. It 's Bertrand Russell on the theory of the atom."

He cleared his throat. It was a book, he said, that he would read with pleasure. The atom was an interesting subject. A very interesting subject. He was glad that she had let him know.

He told her this in heavy whispers, as though the room were filled with sleepers and the hour late.

"There 's no one in the building," she suggested. "I don't think you need to talk that way."

He agreed that this was true.   It was
the force of habit in that room.

For a moment he looked down, and Lucy
Wallis sent her glance along with his.   She
could n't read the title of his book.   It lay
upon its face, as if it, too, considered safety
lay in numbers.

It was more than she had planned, but
she drew a chair up to the table.   "You
read a great deal, don't you?" she observed.

"I like to read when I can find good
books," he said.   "And then, you see, I
don't know many people here."

She nodded.—Did he see that she was
sitting down?   He was still standing there
behind his straight-backed chair, and seemed
to be deciding whether he could roll his eye-
shade flat enough to make it lie inside a
pocket.

"There 's nothing like a good book," she

agreed. "So many people waste their time. Dancing every night, and moving pictures."

She was wondering if he ever danced. What did he think of picture shows?

He kept his feet well on the highway of a literary conversation. "Of course, teaching in the public schools, I have to read a good deal, anyway," he said. "Sort of keep abreast of things, you know."

There was a sandy lock of hair that hung down on his forehead. Probably, she thought, if he did n't comb it straight so often it would curl.

"What do you read most nights in here?" she asked him.

"Oh—different things. I go out in the stacks and find them."

"I know," she said. "I 've seen you. You 're about the only one who comes in here and picks out his own books.

Most people ask me where to find them."

He looked his guilt. "Of course, if there's a rule——"

"Oh, no. There is n't any rule. Most people just don't know which way the numbers go."

"I see. I rather like to hunt around myself. I read different sorts of things, you see. And sometimes I don't know just what I want until I see the title."

"Don't you?" She was surprised at that. "You always look as if you had your mind made up. I mean, when you go out there to the stack-room. I 've always thought— I 've thought when I was sitting at the desk and saw you—that you knew just what you wanted from the start."

"I like to look around a little, first. I guess you know the way I mean. I 've noticed you do quite a bit of reading, too."

He had observed that much, at any rate,

she thought. That eye-shade must be made with a transparent brim.

"You see, I don't know many people either," she suggested.—His hair would be presentable enough if he would comb it right.—"And then, it's a treat to read something worth while now and then. You know, most people who come in here for books read fiction all the time. The lightest sort of fiction. After I've been helping them hunt stories all day long I like to do a little reading of my own."

"Philosophy? That sort of thing?"

She nodded.

"That's fine," he said. "There's nothing like a book to keep your mind on edge. I don't meet many people of that sort out here."

She smiled. Perhaps this much would do them for a starter. She rose, and pushed the chair back to the table.

"I 'm glad you told me of that book," he told her. "What was it—atoms, I believe you said?"

"Yes. Bertrand Russell.—And would you mind if I said something? I like to talk with people who really care for books— I mean, books that matter."

He nodded; cleared his throat again, and stretched his wings to pay her back the compliment.

She left him, went back to her desk, took out her book again. Across the room he buckled on his eye-shade.

Together, while the clock ticked, they sat reading.

He, "The Girl of the Limberlost."

She, the desert story of "The Sheik."

MYRON DAW

I

THEY used to say that Myron Daw would hurdle into fame some morning with a novel well worth writing. But it was a long time before his first bit of fiction saw the printed page.

He had grown up in a print-shop, Myron Daw: playing with slugs of head-line type instead of Noah's Arks, and planning a six-foot shelf of frontier tales at a time when boys his age look forward usually to life as locomotive engineers. Myron's father was old Matthew Daw, who traced his lineage to a drummer-boy at Valley Forge and came to Centerville in 1870 or thereabouts to found the "Star." He was a good printer,

156

Matthew, and a man with high ambitions for his son. Two better years than average in the shop on Market Street, plus what the boy could earn with odd jobs on the side, had sent young Myron off to college. It was there they told him he could write.

He liked writing. He had always liked it. And in these college years his tutors found a certain talent in the work he tried. He did n't aim at anybody's style, but had a certain knack of sketching in detail enough to give his pictures three dimensions. He found it fun to get inside the people in his stories, and did n't bother much with plot. When he dropped his classes in his junior year, to go back home and take his father's place, they told him he deserved to give himself a chance to see what he could do.

He meant to. He would use the "Star," he said, to earn a living—and do his writing on the side. The "Star" was always good for daily bread: a four-page paper, issued twice a week, and fairly stable in its income. It was a modest plant that Myron Daw took over. But it had a press that was n't altogether out of date—and a gas motor, pride of his father's heart, that got the paper printed without broken backs: toll, in the old days, for its contribution to the city's culture.

Myron Daw came home and fed the press fresh copy. From Martin's drug store to the corn-patch just behind St. Mary's Church, all Centerville would know what hour and what day he got his motor running. It would bark three times, and miss; bark three times again. It drowned the noise of wagons in the street, and shook the corn-patch with its echo. Nothing else that the elder Daw bequeathed his son was half so noisily aggressive. There were two antique hand-presses sometimes used for job-work. They watched the door like iron mastiffs; but their bark was as inoffensive as their bite.

It was the motor-driven press that set the pace for the younger Daw when he came home from college; its flapping belts stretched half-way from the rear wall to the rusty stove. The whole plant occupied a single room, low-roofed and crowded, pungent with the ink smell of every printer's shop from Centerville to Kashmir. For the rest: racks of type and stone-topped tables; a chipped mirror on the wall; a clock surmounted by a golden crow; two rows of hooks for hanging galley-proof; a dark towel on a roller never made to roll, wet with the ink of countless adverbs.

Walk up Market Street on Wednesday, and the corn-field slept in peace. But turn the corner on a Friday or a Monday, and two blocks distant came the news of Centerville on wings of short impatient snorts.

II

It was in the first year following his father's death, when he was still in his early twenties, and perhaps a little young for the adventure, that Myron Daw set out to write his novel.

Something of an epic he had planned. They told him at the university that America was a land without a cultural tradition: no folk-lore—a sharp line cutting off the red men from the whites who drove them west—successive layers of immigration spread on top of one another like new frostings on a baker's-window cake. Very well. Let that be granted. We had something else instead. We had freedom. Not freedom, perhaps, in the sense of something well achieved. But freedom from the dead. His tale would catch the spirit that exults in twenty-story buildings rising overnight where yesterday was just a hole—of mammoth furnaces in Allegheny hills that clamor greedily for ore dug far away in Minnesota and rushed from earth to polished steel with circus speed—of iron cities hammered out in one short generation from frontier towns with trading-posts and forts.

That would be his theme. And in these first days of his return to Centerville neighbors used to stop him on the streets sometimes to ask about his progress. When would he have his novel ready to be printed? Daw would explain that the writing of a tale takes time. However, he had started work, he said. And that was true. He had sketched his chapters in rough form on squares of red and yellow cardboard: and played a game of shifting them to suit his fancy. Here and there he tried a bit of text. He liked especially one spot in which an iron-master trumpeted the swift march of iron conquest, and wrote it several times. "Take that hulking town, Chicago. Do you know that forty years ago it was a place of less than twenty thousand people? Do you know that then the seepage from the East had spent itself in Indiana prairies —that stage-coach trusts were fighting the first railways—that farmers thought plank roads could beat a locomotive to the Lakes?"

And more. He liked the way he meant to bring that passage in; he had other favorites. But it was hard to push the thing along; the "Star" was always hungry for his time.

For the "Star" had no reporters. It had

no pressmen. The staff consisted of Daw himself, his sister, and Ed Tate. His sister set the type; Tate helped her; but tender years and an unerring eye for picking *v* when he wanted *w* made Tate's contribution somewhat meager. For the rest, the work of gathering news and printing it belonged to Daw himself.

Nor was that all. Myron Daw, in this first year, was busy trying innovations. No reform in city politics or civic culture seemed too thoroughgoing then. Daw was ready for them all. He thought up city slogans to be run in giant type. He organized "campaigns." He led the volunteers in every skirmish. He did n't stop with that; he took the "Star," so satisfactory to his father for a span of fifteen years, and shook it till its ancient head-lines rattled.

He did n't like its advertisements.

Lame backs and twisted torsos, most of
them; in a mighty train, equipped with testi-
monials of fortunate recovery, came Gude's
Rheumatic Powders, Lady's Distemper
Compound; Vito, Old Reliable Heartburn
Capsules, Co-San for Bronchitis. Daw
tried to drum up local trade to take the
place of patent medicines. It did n't come.
Stores in Centerville were so well known to
every one in town, and for the most part had
so little competition, that public adver-
tisement in the press comprised a luxury to
be indulged in only after due reflection.
Myron Daw made little headway with his
local clientele; and in the end, because it
was either that or shut up shop, he kept Co-
San and all its colleagues where they were
—and comforted himself with the reflection
that no one took these magic claims at their
face-value: therefore, whether they ap-

peared or disappeared, was not a matter of importance.

Besides, he told himself, there were other changes well worth making first. He would give the "Star" a front page that really carried news.

That front page, as the elder Daw had planned it, consisted largely of home gossip. "Solons Argue Paving Bids."—"Rift in Presbyterian Choir."—Occasionally an item from the outside world would force itself out here among the leaders: when some one sent a Christmas turkey to the White House, or a shark was sighted at Palm Beach. But the ratio was usually one to twenty: with Centerville at twenty, and the rest of the wide world at one.

All this the younger Daw upturned. He put the wide world on his outside page— with Centerville tucked well between the covers. He made the change; stuck to it for six weeks; but found his patrons did n't like it. The town could read world news in papers from the city, forty miles away— and only liked the "Star" because it featured Centerville.

A second time this son turned back and took his father's counsel. The one sure way to keep your readers on the list, old Matthew Daw had said, was to get them into print at least one week in every six.

A social note with twenty names was better copy than a battle.

III

Time passed. The elder Daw had been at rest perhaps five years. The "Star," as published by his son and heir, stood just about where he had left it.

And the novel?

Going slower now. Once or twice a year he sorted out his cardboard chapters; mulled them over; rearranged them. But he added no new sections. In fact, he threw out two or three that he had done before. His one new contribution was to print a title in red letters on the cover of a note-book. Letters inches high; the short word, "DAWN." It looked well; and the note-book, he decided, was a good idea. He could carry it with him to the office in the morning; bring it home at night; write a page or two each day.

He carried it to the office. He even brought it home again at night. He carried it to the office a second time. And then he left it; but he did n't write. The day's routine was too absorbing. And the "Star," to tell the truth, was too much fun. More and more did Myron Daw begin to take an interest in that first page of his, to the exclusion of all other ventures.

There were paragraphs that might be written, slyly poking fun at some good-humored neighbor: paragraphs that would produce a sheepish grin next day, on Market Street, and an admission, willingly imparted, "Well Myron, you certainly put it over on me *that* time."

There were other paragraphs that could flick with the lash of satire some culprit richly meriting rebuke; other paragraphs: to welcome into the world a new-born babe, and (let it be admitted) brings its grandfather to the office with a half-dollar for ten extra copies of the paper. Still others to come cantering to the defense of anybody accused of anything, at any time, on the general principle that a man in trouble needs a friend. Others: patting on the back some obscure guardian in a rôle still more obscure, faithful to a humdrum job. "Letting that gate drop where the C. L. & B. crosses Maple Street is n't anything for a Napoleon. But when you 've watched that gate for thirty years and never had a smash-up, and count the times you could have done it wrong and all the winter nights you 've frozen in a little two-by-four watch-tower, there are some things in life you don't need to be ashamed of. John Meigs rounds out his thirtieth year to-morrow. We 're going out and hang a sprig of apple-blossoms on his weather-beaten barrier."

Not much importance in all this, as the affairs of planets go. But a major item for a man who 's watched a gate for thirty years, or finds himself put to it for a friend, or wants the farthest reaches of the universe to know he has a grandson.

Centerville would turn the pages of the "Star," and laugh or rage or praise with

Myron Daw.   Somewhere, no doubt, you 'd
have found a college tutor who remembered
him.   "Daw?   Certainly   I   recall   him.
Odd   name,   you   know.   Bright   young   fellow.   Wanted   to   write.

"Might   have   had   real   influence   if   he 'd
stuck to it."

IV

How   long   it   had   been,   when   a   certain
morning came in spring, since Myron Daw
had   written   a   chapter   of   the   novel   that   was
going to carry him to fame—or even, if the
truth be known, so much as laid his eyes
upon the red letters of his note-book cover—
probably not even the man himself was sure.
Certainly   a   good   many   years.   Time   had
given   the   editor   of   the   "Star"   a   pair   of
stooping shoulders, clipped six inches from
his stride.   Myron Daw was fifty-five.

Not that fifty-five meant settling down.
He would eat lunch at the depot counter
when the morning still seemed young.
Sometimes, when a new idea popped into his
head, he would bolt from the place at such
a clip that not for half a block would he
remember his hat was hanging on a peg
above the paper towels. Stop him on the
street, and he would punctuate his sentences
with swift digs into a waistcoat pocket for
his watch. He would light a cigar with the
genial idlers who kept Tom Creavy's auto-
matic lighter spurting jets of well-tamed
flame; but he was gone before the ash had
lengthened to the flicking-point.

"Beats all!" Tom Creavy would observe.
"You 'd think he 'd have enough of it by this
time."

"What 's he up to now?"

"No telling." Tom would put away the
tray of panetelas, tidy up the matches in the

cracker-box. "Like as not he's thought of some hot shot to give the mayor, or maybe he remembers he's misspelled a word on the third page of that precious paper. That paper! The whole sun rises in that paper. And sets, too. Yes, sir, rises and sets, too, in that paper." Tom would snap back the latch of his cigar-case, pour a little water on the sponge. "It certainly beats all."

But Myron Daw, on this special after-noon in spring, was off neither for a hot shot at the mayor nor to catch a printer's error in the paper. He remembered an old friend coming home—and thought that on the top shelf of his office closet he had stored a pic-ture worth reprinting.

There, in a heap of dust that hid old type and 3-em spaces, he found a heap of red and yellow cardboards—and a tattered note-book labelled "DAWN."

"Make a point," the first card told him, "of the fact that it is *youth* that gets things done . . . iron cities hammered out in one short generation from frontier towns with trading-posts and forts."

Youth? . . . Yes, youth. No doubt of that. But where had he put that picture? . . . A card escaped him, and came swirling down. He picked it up. "Do you know," he read, "that forty years ago Chicago was a little town of less than twenty thousand people? Do you know that then the seepage from the East had spent itself in Indiana prairies—that stage-coach trusts were fighting the first railways—that farmers thought plank roads could beat a locomotive to the Lakes?"

"That's interesting," thought Myron Daw. "Just change the date and use it now. Handy little filler. . . . Wish I could locate that picture."

He dusted off the card.   They used to say that Myron Daw would hurdle into fame some morning with a novel well worth writing.   But not until that afternoon in spring did his first bit of fiction see the light of day.

MILLIE TURNER

I

CARTER HAYES, who went to the city now and then to hear an opera, used to say that Millie Turner was another Madame Butterfly. You can judge for yourself if their stories are alike. But remember Carter's opera was all commuting, and he missed the final act.

Millie Turner was a waitress when this chapter of her life began. She worked behind the counter in the depot lunch-room of the C. L. & B. She did n't have the olive eyes and oriental grace of Cho-Cho-San. But she was young, slim, pert, and even-tempered—with a pair of eyes of such a thought-suspending blue that more than one incoming passenger in a rush for coffee and a slice of ham forgot his haste and stayed for porter-house, french fried, and custard cake before his meal was done.   Millie's hair was black, a midnight black; she combed it flat across her head with a thin gleam of white skin up the center, and a Spanish comb stuck up behind as rakishly as if the sign-board on this station read "Seville."   Some-times No. 9, which stops at Centerville to let its passengers dismount for lunch, would have to whistle twice to get the male contin-gent back again.   "Don't care *how* much they   eat,"   the   brakeman   would   ob-serve.   "East-bound local!   Hillside, Cres-ton, Church's Ferry, Walbridge, Endicott —east-bound local, all abo-o-o-ard!"

More than likely Millie Turner's charms were rated at full value by patrons of the line.   There were traveling salesmen who came this way on principle, whenever shirts

or overshoes could bring them within strik-
ing distance of the town. In the station
Judson Clark, the baggage-man, was no
better than the rest of them. He used to
keep his ticket-punch in a drawer of Millie
Turner's counter, so that he could come out
there to get it when a trunk arrived. Even
old Sam Cole, the station-master, the one
redeeming feature of whose job it was to dis-
pose of tickets as unobligingly as possible
and snap back, "Look it up in the time-table
—what 're your eyes for," if customers asked
him when a train was due, would lock the
brass bars of his window and come from his
cage with a face that was wreathed in smiles,
to get his luncheon.

If ever a railway-station had a queen,
Millie Turner sat on the throne in Centerville. And like a queen she took this ad-
miration lightly. Too sternly virtuous, her
suitors found her. But old Sam Cole took

note, and his colleague in the baggage-room might likewise have observed, had his own eyes not been so dimmed by his infatuation, that there was one traveler upon whom Millie Turner looked with animation. East-bound No. 7, which goes through Centerville at 11:36 A. M. and comes back west as No. 32 at supper-time, was more important than most trains. In its engine-cabin rode a curly-headed fireman.

For a year or two he 'd had this run: a young fellow of twenty-eight or thereabouts —rather quiet; handsome in an offhand way; trade-marked with his job by streaks of coal-dust on his cheeks and just behind his ears; a red handkerchief tucked in around a throat that Rodin might have chiseled from a somewhat dirty stone. Up and down the line he was a favorite; but Centerville was his only port of call. Before the brakes had caught he 'd swing himself aground, and with momentum borrowed from the wheels come charging to the station. Woe betide the hungry on Trains 32 and 7. Millie Turner had no time for traveling salesmen now. She 'd lean across the counter, blue eyes sparkling like the polished handles on her coffee-urn, and watch this yellow-headed god of hers eat pie.

Lemon custard he liked best. Millie would start to get it ready when 32 began to whistle in the yards, a soup-plate upside down on top of it to keep the flies away. Loungers in the lunch-room did n't have much doubt that Millie was "Jim Holden's girl." You could tell, they said, from the way she looked at him when he came coasting in. Jim Holden lived two stations up the line. He came to Centerville on Fridays; that was his off day for the week; and sometimes, when she could get her sister to fill in for her, Millie would go away with

him.   They 'd use a railway pass and try the
city for a vaudeville in winter-time—go
down to Lake Grove Park in summer for an
evening on the roller-coaster.   One time, in
spring, they went to the city, shopping.
Jim would n't let his lady look when they
went in the jeweler's store.   It was a tie-
clasp he wanted, he declared; his four-in-
hand was always coming loose and flapping
in his face.   They had those little clamps
with teeth on them that bit into the goods.

But when they left the store again Jim
brought a ring with him.   "Look here!   It
did n't cost so much," he said in self-defense.
"They 've got a sale on now.   And maybe
you can find some place to put the thing."

That was the way Jim Holden sought a
bride.   Next day when Millie Turner
brought the waffles to her guests, a sparkle
on one finger broke the news.

II

Madame Butterfly, if you remember, did n't know until one morning when she saw a strange white woman in the garden that her lover had another wife. Millie Turner had more luck. She heard of that before the day arrived when she 'd agreed to marry Jim.

There is something odd about the history of No. 7. The yardmen call it an unlucky train. It had scarcely got up steam that morning, eastward bound, when a stray passenger who had been struggling at the ticket-window with the buttons of his overcoat came back across the room. It was cold, he said. He 'd like a cup of coffee. The prospect of refreshment seemed to put him in good cheer. Strange the way you met people when you did n't expect it, he observed. He went on struggling with his coat. Now take that young fireman, for instance: the fellow who 'd been standing here. He had n't thought of him in years. Used to know him in the city. Neighbors then. That was before the fellow quarreled with his wife. She living down here now? Quite a well-appearing woman—nice hair, though maybe not her own. Folks said she had a temper though. Well, how long did people have to wait for coffee in this place? Coffee. Coffee! C-o- double f-e-e. What was so interesting to look at through that window, anyway?

It was casual enough. Millie Turner found herself believing she had heard all this before. Jim found the ring between two plates when 32 came back that evening. He was straight enough about it. Of course he 'd meant to clear it up, he said, before he married Millie—he meant to do it now.

Eight years ago he'd married. "She had a big red hat—it'd been raining—the red ran down her hair." He was a youngster at the time; nineteen, or maybe twenty. They'd lived together for a year. It might have been his fault as much as hers they'd quarreled; he wasn't hanging medals on himself. But she'd packed her clothes— they had a bedroom in a boarding-house— and gone away one noon. It was six months or so before he'd heard from her. She was out west with her brother then. She'd told him to forget it; she was through. She didn't need his money; her brother had had a run of luck, and she'd be square enough to tell him so. Seven years. He'd let things slide; you know the way it goes. A man can forget a lot of things in seven years; not just forget them, maybe, but sort of not remember they're his own. He ought to have started out to settle things

before he ever spoke to Millie. No doubt
of that; of course he meant to do it now——

Jim Holden was no man for eloquence.
Millie always did the talking for them both.
Easier, Jim thought, to get up steam on a
stone-cold locomotive than tell a girl about
your worries or your dreams. But this time,
while No. 32 was marking time to take on
freight, Jim Holden got a story off his chest
without a waste of words.

He had taken off his neck-piece now, and
stood there wrapping up the ring.

"I won't be back until it's straight," he
told her. "You'll be waiting when I
come?"

"You come first," she answered, "and
you'll see."

III

They brought a prince to Madame Butterfly when her lieutenant went away. He was

an old man; but he was well-to-do and ready
to be married. Madame Butterfly preferred to wait. Millie Turner had no
prince; but princes do not travel on the
C. L. & B., and Millie might have had a
traveling salesman if she 'd wanted
one.

It was easy at first to wait for Jim.
There were days when it almost seemed as
if she ought to have her bag packed. She 'd
get a postal now and then: Jim had gone
west to see his wife and settle things. There
would come a panorama of the City Hall or
Fairbanks Park, with a finely scribbled message on its three-eighths inch of margin.
It had rained a lot, or the nights were cold,
or the city was a hard place to get used to.
Millie kept those cards in a Pullman envelope. Jim had been a generous spender;
but he had n't gone in for treasures that
would last. Postal cards were all she had

that ever had belonged to him. Postal cards and lemon pies.

A man who liked that yellow cream as well as Jim did was bound to be remembered when the baker's boy came whistling in the morning. And for a time, whenever custard tops seemed extra thick or extra fine, Millie felt she'd like to put a piece aside where Jim could get it in the evening. She knew that would n't do; the crust would be like boxwood when he got there. But then, you could n't tell; he might be planning to surprise her.

Train No. 32, and its companion, 7, mattered less as time went by. What counted was the day's adventure with the postman. "Nothing to-day," he would tell her, most of the time, "but just pour me out a cup of coffee, will you? Cold as blazes, out of doors." Coffee every morning, and more cups between each post-card. Millie would wonder what Jim's wife looked like, and hope the streak of red from her wedding hat was there to stay, while she leaned an elbow on the counter and slid her guest the sugar-bowl. Jim's sugar-bowl. And everybody's else. A deceptive coating of loose grains on lumps as hard as stone, the residue of countless dippings with wet spoons.

By and by the post-cards stopped. Millie did n't know it at the time. The only way you know a thing like that is to look back on it afterward. Two months between. Three months. Five. Then a gentle fade-away. Sometimes, from the engineman on 32, Millie would hear a bit of news; Jim had fallen in with some old friend, or joined a lodge, or found a job railroading in the West. A steady job? One that was going to keep him there? "He did n't say."

It took a lot of time for weeks and months

to stow themselves away.   Slowly this out-post of the C. L. & B. changed hands.   Judson Clark, in the baggage-room, moved out of town one spring and brought a daughter with him when he came back home again. Old Sam Cole rode away one night in a baggage-car, to a town for which he 'd sold ten thousand round-trip tickets in his time. Millie Turner shined her cups and spoons and watched the years go by.

Only now and then, when No. 7 began to whistle for a clear track through the yards, she 'd find her hands down at her sides, her eyes fixed on the door.

"East-bound   local—Hillside,   Creston, Church's Ferry, Walbridge, Endicott—all abo-o-ard!"

IV

When Pinkerton came back to Madame Butterfly she 'd heard the guns down in the harbor and knew that he was on his way. Millie Turner just looked up from a plate of ham and eggs one night and saw Jim Holden at the door.

She was another Millie Turner when that moment came. A plump Millie—who would have predicted it, at thirty-five?—and she could n't dart across the room the way she used to meet him; but in a moment she was at his side.

"Well, Millie, here we are again." He smiled. "Say, anybody 'd think you saw a ghost." He took her hand.

Jim back! She had n't expected it this way. How long had he been gone? He 's heavier, she thought. And something 's different with his eyes. What had happened to that curly hair? The fringes left above his ears were thin and straight.

"Jim, where 's your wife?"

"I buried her last fall." His eyes

dropped to the counter. "You see, I stuck it out. I just did n't get around to breaking with her when I got back again. I thought I could, but I sort of put it off at first—and after that it was too late."

He had let go her hand, and was fumbling in his waistcoat pocket.

"And now?" she asked.

"Well, I've saved a little money now," he said, "and I sort of thought I'd try the East a while. You know. The time comes when a fellow likes a change."

"Children?"

He shook his head.

"You'll go alone?"

"Well, *maybe* not alone. You see, I kind of thought——"

She knew what it was he kind of thought, but it did n't hold her interest. She was thinking now of a story she had read. A girl was waiting in a tower for one of those fellows who used to go to war in iron suits. Years, she 'd been waiting there: and the fellow never guessed it.

She wiped two hands that were red and fat upon her apron. Then she shook her head. "No, Jim," she said.

Outside, No. 6 or No. 9 or No. 32—with a start it came to her that after all these years she could n't remember right this minute which was which—stood waiting on the tracks while freight was being dumped aboard its baggage-car.

Jim seemed to have found what he 'd been looking for, but put it back again.

"Millie, you would n't come along with me?" he asked.

She shook her head.

"I 'm free," he told her.

Free? Maybe so. But not free the way a curly-headed Jim was free. To middle age or indecision, to some dead love or some dead dream, she told herself that he was chained.

A door opened. It seemed a long time before a brakeman had his head inside. "East-bound local—ready now! Hillside, Creston, Church's Ferry, Walbridge, Endicott, and points east. Abo-o-rd!"

HARVEY BURCH

I

WHEN he was a lad in grammar-school Harvey Burch liked Hallowe'en. He used to wrap himself in a tattered sheet, cut eye-holes in a pillow-slip, and hide in the shadow of the old board fence behind the Baptist Church. When people passed the alleyway he'd jump out with an unexpected "Boo!" That was thirty years ago. Now Harvey was a Kleagle.

There was no Klan in his small town. Centerville had yet to see the bright gleam of the flaming cross. But there was a corps of knights in Auburn, seven miles away; and Harvey was a full-fledged member: white, Protestant, and native-born—oath sworn and name inscribed upon the roster. This time he paid ten dollars for his pillow-slip. But Hallowe'en came several times a year; Harvey did n't need to wait for an October night to hide behind the church and scare the passer-by.

He was a man of thirty-eight or thirty-nine, this Klansman: not the type you 'd pick instinctively to represent the domineering Anglo-Saxon. His face was peacefully at repose in its pale features: chin and forehead both receding from an upturned nose. His chest was shallow. His arms were short; so short, in fact, that he had to stand on a chair to reach the third shelf in Martin's drug store, where, in interludes between his Klan activities, he earned his daily bread. When he paraded in the evening with his fellow-Klansmen it was with a row of safety-pins around his legs, to keep the long white robe from trailing on the ground.

Sixteen years it had been, since Harvey Burch first climbed a ladder to the upper shelves. He was as much a part of Martin's store as the old-fashioned scales on which its customers discovered whether they were losing weight. Prescriptions were beyond his depth; George Martin, the proprietor, looked after those; but there was not a box of cough-drops or a cake of perfumed soap, a tube of tooth-paste or a loose bolt in the ancient soda-water fountain, with whose cost and purpose he was not on friendly terms.

"Mrs. Blake was in to-day," he would tell his family at supper. "Took some of that new laundry soap, three bars for a quarter. I guess Henry Trench must have another earache. His wife bought some of Colby's

ointment in the store to-day.   Large box.
The dollar size.   I sold Ned Frye a forty-
nine-cent tooth-brush."

A conscientious workman, faithful to his
trade; and within the limits of the salary a
man can earn by mixing sundaes seven
days a week, a good father to his boys.
Harvey Burch had two of them.   One six,
the other nine.   They were quiet youngsters, in whose presence Harvey felt at times
a little shy.   Only once had either lad been
made to feel the heavy hand of justice.
That was on a certain Sunday afternoon,
when the elder son had found a limp white
garment hidden in the pantry closet, and
borrowed it for a parade around the block.
Harvey spied him from a window of the
drug store, and met him at the corner with a
brush.

For there are certain secrets not intended
even for one's son and heir.   It was always

with a modest show of mystery that Harvey started for his secret meetings—a vague description of his future whereabouts, and a careful wrapping of his night-robe in the manila bag brought home at supper-time. But his wife knew well enough, when her ordinarily out-spoken husband began to look like Cesare Borgia doctoring his guests' dessert, that Harvey Burch and his manila bag were on their way to Auburn. Somewhere, before the night was over, the flaming cross would blaze again.

That worried her.   One time in a moving-picture show she 'd seen a horde of Klansmen charging on their horses through the broken fields.   That was all she knew about the Klan; but it was enough to remind her of the fact that Harvey had never learned to ride.

One pilgrimage to Auburn might have reassured her.   Horses had no share in this adventure. Auburn Klansmen rode in Fords. The greatest risk her husband ran was sitting in his night-robe on the grass.

II

Walk into Martin's drug store in the afternoon; note the never-failing courtesy with which its clerk invited you to take advantage of some special bargain—the interest he displayed in any possible purchase you might make—the discriminating eye with which he counseled you upon the merits of competing talcums—and you would have found it difficult to believe that this mild-mannered man was either friend or foe of Law and Order. It is a long way from the soda-fountain to the lions' den. But never a more enthusiastic Klansman.

There had been a certain short, imposing stranger who arrived in town one afternoon, and over a tray of hair-dyes on the counter confided that he 'd like to plan a rendezvous with Harvey Burch that evening. To be sure, the rendezvous turned out to have no more exciting background than Mrs. Poulter's boarding-house in Vine Street; but it was there that the quiet stranger proved, with page on page of documents, that the country was menaced by a three-forked danger; nothing but the Ku Klux Klan could save the nation from its fate.

There are men who carry chips, and challenge all the world to knock them off; but Harvey Burch walked the streets of life with a peril on his shoulder. Facts that most men took at something like face-value he would multiply by four. When he had shared a paper with some customer, and read about a storm down state, he was ready for the next man with a cyclone. Perils were the things he lived for, as some men 'live for risk and others for gold. You'd find, if you sat next to him when the circus came to town, that he was just inclined to think the bars were n't strong enough to hold the Bengal tiger.

Harvey asked for details. His friend was ready to supply them. Here were photographs, he said, of secret orders—transcripts of a conversation certain parties overheard. Here were sworn copies of the testimony——

The quiet stranger heaped his transcripts and his photographs on one of Mrs. Poulter's bedroom tables. Harvey Burch remarked the fact that there seemed to be no end of evidence, but wondered, when it came to confidential interviews, at the reason for his own selection.

Because, his friend confided, he was recommended by a certain "X" in Auburn.

The name of "X" was whispered. Harvey knew him? Yes.

After all, dispensing talcums is an unexciting trade. Harvey Burch did not object to something with a touch of the crusader in the evening. And certainly "Hail, Kleagle!" sounded satisfying to an ear attuned to "Two vanilla sodas, please."

Harvey pledged himself to the payment of an entrance-fee before the week was out. He would be a Kleagle, once he had a Klan. For the present, his mentor told him, he 'd be carried on the Auburn roster: Auburn was a factory town, with the movement in full swing.

He left the boarding-house. A little strange, this new adventure. Vine Street looked the way it always had.

Still, that fellow had it right. Trouble in the air. Crime waves—prices going up—

and unrest everywhere. Somebody must have started it.

When anything unpleasant happens, the Harvey Burches of the world look underneath the bed.

III

A menace does n't look the same when you can call it Jim or Harry. It 's the nameless terrors that cast mighty shadows.

Search-lights from a score of motors lit a hollow square with light. White-robed figures marched and countermarched with torch-lights. Harvey Burch had been a Klansman for six weeks.

He had come to Auburn with a new manila bag. He had met the challenge of the sentinel, and caught his long robe at the knees as a precaution against stumbling on uneven ground—to-night's conclave chose a corn-patch treacherous with stubble; and now he stood on a small hillock for its better view, and watched new Klansmen being led before the flag-draped Bible. Lost waifs toiling the Elysian fields: from a dozen unexpected quarters they were halted, challenged, cross-examined; made to kneel, and made to rise; pledged, plighted, covenanted, sworn by all that 's holy. Harvey Burch contributed his own ringing "Aye!" upon proper signal to the chorus— lifted his voice in a hymn that carried out across the corn-patch to the rolling meadows —shielded his eyes from the gasolene-soaked cross that flared up unexpectedly— and raced through ranks of churning motors for a ride with some one bound for Center-ville. He found a dry-goods man from Prescott who would drop him on the way.

"*Some* turnout, eh?" his new friend asked.

"*Some* turnout!"

"Certainly makes a man feel great—hullo! there 's a fellow from my town—feel great, I say, to see so many fellows showing up for duty."

"Certainly does," said Harvey.

"Have n't started things in your town have they?"

"Not yet. I 'm Kleagle, but it 's pretty slow."

"I know. Those little towns are sleepy. Don't realize the situation."

"Exactly what I tell them!" Harvey said. "Can't make them see the danger."

"But it 's there," his friend observed. "Just hold that match a minute, will you?"

"You bet it 's there!" said Harvey. "I don't mind saying I was a little skeptical when I went into this. Just sort of thought I 'd have a look around, you know. But the more I see, the more I understand just what we 're up against.—Here, let me take it and I'll light it for you.—Just what we're up against, you know. Do you realize there are three million Jews in the United States? And eight—it's either eight or ten—ten million niggers? By George, the deeper you get into this thing the more it strikes you as appalling.

"Of course—" Harvey Burch paused to light his friend's cigar—"when I talk to some of the boys this way—you know, the likely ones for members—they say, 'Yes, but what's all that to *us?*' They don't understand, you see. You've got to draw the line somewhere. And the place, *I* say, is right up at the start. Now, I was reading yesterday——"

IV

The car from Prescott pulled up at the curb, dropped Harvey Burch, and went its way.

Ten thirty. Too late, he thought, for a game of cribbage with his neighbor on the right. These Ku Klux nights played hob with cribbage. He used to meet that neighbor at the board five times a week. For years they 'd played together. Never Sundays: Harvey would n't break the Lord's Day. Never Saturdays: this friend across the alleyway was orthodox in his religion, as well as hustling in his trade. He kept the Jewish Sabbath.

Harvey crossed the narrow lawn. He climbed the low steps to his porch; unlocked the door; then slipped the key beneath the mat. The key was meant for Sam.

Risky, to let this coal-black truckman roam the house for garden tools, an hour before daybreak? Oh, no. Sam risky? Shucks! who would n't give a key to Sam?

It 's the nameless terrors that cast mighty

shadows. When you can call it Jim or Harry, a menace does n't look the same.

But that was n't the thought in Harvey Burch's mind, as he turned out the light and groped his way along the hall to hide his night-robe on a closet shelf.

Thirty years ago a small boy used to hide behind the Baptist Church and hop out with an unexpected "Boo!" When he was a lad in grammar-school, there was one holiday that Harvey Burch ranked well ahead of Santa Claus and Christmas.

Hallowe'en.

JIM LEE

I

IT is against the code to naturalize an alien Oriental. But Centerville found a way of settling that. Jim Lee came to his own with a McKinley button.

There was a little shop well toward the eastern end of Market Street, where Jim Lee ran a Chinese laundry. You opened the door and crowded past a wicker basket heaped with linen. A sheaf of enigmatic Chinese letters fluttered on pink strips; Jim Lee would be standing there, behind the counter, with an iron in his hand. His face defied the seasons. Impossible to guess what he was thinking; impossible to tell how old he was. Willis Bender's guess was seventeen; Harvey Peeke thought sixty-six would be more likely.

Jim would put the iron in its rack, look up, and wait for your commands. He spoke little English; but that little was concise, and admirably clear. Nevertheless, once across this threshold it was difficult not to talk in Pidgin-English. Odd phrases seemed to go with Jim Lee's yellow hands and almond eyes. How else, you felt, could he be made to understand you? "No starch in shirt," you'd say. "No starch. You savvy?"

Jim Lee would nod. "You want the cuffs soft?"

"Cuffs allee-samee soft. No starch, you savvy?"

Jim Lee would roll the unstarched shirt and stick a long pink ticket on it; then hand you back what might have said, for all your knowledge of this complicated script, "Well scorched." You left the little shop in Market Street with some pleasure in the fact you'd proved yourself a linguist.

People liked Jim Lee. His quiet mask was interesting. He had lived in Centerville four years, and suffered little loss in novelty. He would always look the same, the town was sure, no matter what might come to pass inside him. No one had ever seen him alter his expression. Ned Frye heard him cry out with what seemed to be a high-pitched Chinese oath, one evening when a red-hot iron toppled over on his fingers. But his face, on that occasion, had retained the same impassive smile with which he took your white duck trousers and suggested "Monday."

He wore no cue—Jim Lee. His hair was barbered in the style affected by his patrons. Nor was there anything in his choice of clothes that marked him as an

Oriental. He liked what Market Street re-
garded as the latest thing, and seemed, when
he left his shop, to want to merge himself
with the rest of Centerville. Work kept
him fairly well employed. Most of the
town's washing, to be sure, was done in cellar laundries by industrious wives; but there
were single men who found Jim Lee a useful institution. His work was clean, and it
was prompt; and it was inexpensive. His
best friends were men who brought their
shirts and collars to him: Ira Niles and
Harvey Peeke and Myron Daw, who edited
the "Star." They would ask him where he
left his pigtail, and what he thought about
mah-jongg, and how he got along without
chop-suey. He liked these customers; and
however little of their wit he understood, he
liked their friendly banter. When they
asked him if it was n't true that the Chinese
nation lived on eggs laid long before the

days of Christopher Columbus, he caught the one word "eggs" and gave them the smile he had showed Ned Frye the night he burned his fingers on the iron.

For the rest, Jim Lee had little save work to keep him entertained.   He had no fellow-countrymen in town; he ironed shirts—sent home the major portion of his earnings—and indulged himself in a stately walk on Sunday afternoons.   Men like Myron Daw were sometimes heard to speak his praise. No better citizen on Market Street, said Myron; he believed the fellow would like to call himself a native, if he could, and just settle down.   One word he 'd learned somewhere was "citizen."   Sometimes got his dates mixed—but a good patriot, just the same; Myron had seen him hanging up a flag, one Christmas evening.

Willis Bender had the same opinion, but there were other neighbors not so sure.   It was rumored, for one thing, that Jim Lee's diet was not a thing to talk about in public. It was rumored, again, that he smoked opium in the back room of his laundry, Sunday evenings. The small boys in town were especially certain of that point; and reported, on occasions, they had seen the smoke come curling from his windows in great puffs like burning leaves. That seemed only to be expected, on the whole. Jim Lee was a Chinaman; he would take to opium as naturally as an Italian takes to wine.

Nor was that all. It could n't be forgotten that as an Oriental Jim had no religion. Ned Frye declared he worshiped sticks and stones. Arthur Crosby said he worshiped Brahma. They argued it. Aunt Polly Stearns declared it made no difference which was right—and on one occasion slipped a catechism into the pocket of her brother's coat, when he sent his new pajamas to the laundry.

II

There came a night when it fell to Jim Lee's lot to play the hero modestly. In the office of the "Star," a half-block up the street, two wires crossed; and, with the building empty, a red torch of burning casement lit one wall. Jim Lee had a glimpse of it from the doorway of his laundry—hurried to the scene and broke a window—beat the flame out with a broom.

Myron Daw was on the spot, as soon as the news reached him. The office was a timber building; it would have gone like kindling, he declared. He owed Jim Lee eternal thanks. What could he do, to show he really meant it?

Jim Lee's English was n't up to the oc-

casion. Good as it was, in starch and soaps
and laundry ware, it failed before the test
of conflagrations. He remarked enough,
however, to inform him that his kindly
neighbor offered him a proof of friendship;
and willing to accept the chance in the best
of faith he declared that nothing would suit
him better than for Mr. Daw to make him
a citizen of the country.

Having expected something in the way
of a request for a suit of clothes or a
perpetual contract for his laundry, Daw
found this sudden summons disconcerting.
He suggested, as an alternative, a flat-iron
running on electric current. But Jim Lee
shook his head politely. He hoped to wear
a flag and vote.

There was a law, said Myron Daw, that
forbade such things to happen. Chinese,
like Japanese, could not be naturalized.
Did n't Jim know that?

Jim Lee knew about the law; but men of the omnipotence of Myron Daw, he suggested, had been known to have laws set aside upon occasion.

Jim had no doubts. But Myron Daw was forced to shake his head. Still, it seemed poor courtesy to reject without so much as second thought the first boon claimed by the savior of an uninsured frame building; and so he put off until morning what would be easier to do by light of day.

But Jim Lee was waiting for him in the morning; and before Myron Daw had a chance to press again the claims of the electric iron, Jim told him, in laundry English ill adapted to the tale, but breathlessly, the way he'd come to cherish this idea of adoption.

There were moving pictures in Shanghai; he had caught his first glimpse of America upon the screen. A wondrous land—

where nobody had to pull a rickshaw—since everybody rode around on horseback. Of the slow progress of his pilgrimage—the ship that smuggled sixty of his countrymen across a weather-beaten strip of seacoast, the sudden transformation of Ling Mon-Chang to plain Jim Lee, the fate that led him into Centerville—he had little to relate. But there he was. And while America was not the same exciting land that danced across the motion-picture screen in Shanghai, for all that it remained a noble nation. He had his goal. In one direction lay security and rich content.

The influential Mr. Daw would see him made a citizen.

III

It was Myron Daw's opinion that foreigners are a nuisance generally, and the

Chinese in particular; but he was aware that he might be dealing here with a dream as well worth having as the next man's. And he was inclined to think that from the ritual of being "made a citizen" this quiet friend so skilful with the iron expected to derive a peace of mind quite out of all proportion to its just deserts.

That was Myron's guess. And that may have been the reason why he let himself be jockeyed by his own good humor into the impossible position of telling Jim he 'd see what could be done to waive the law. Impossible—because Myron Daw discovered that this friend of his was not to be put off ultimately with a second choice. So hopefully did Jim Lee wait for news that was n't on its way that Myron Daw chose shortly to avoid the laundry and enticed his sister into washing shirts at home. It did him little good. His sister scorched the only shirt that reached his wrists; and Jim Lee, meantime, began to dog his footsteps to the office. He was not presuming. He never chose to come inside and interrupt the day's routine. But he would wait outside the door an hour for a chance to tip his hat. He would smile ("but then," thought Myron Daw, "the beggar's *always* smiling"); he would look expectantly for some fresh bit of information—watch Myron Daw go past—then fall astern and trail his patron to the corner: to come and wait again to-morrow.

The lonely vigil got on Myron's nerves a little. He asked his sister what she thought about it. She told him he was mad. "Never heard of such a thing!" she hooted. "Afraid to tell a Chinaman you can't change the law for him. Why, Myron Daw, you're loony!"

Myron Daw admitted it. "But then," he said, "you don't know the way he looks at you. So sort of trustful. Oh, well, I 'll tell him in the morning. Might as well just stop this thing. But you 've seen him, Molly, have 'nt you? Comes and waits outside the door. Sometimes when it 's raining. You don't see how I feel about it."

But Myron Daw had another friend who saw. That was Simon Hodge, the doctor. Simon said, "Don't do it."

"Got to."

"Why?"

"What else?"

"Well, I don't know," said Simon Hodge. "You say he 's none too strong on English?"

"Hardly knows a word of it except the laundry business."

"Um-m. . . . Well, there are lots of ways to take an oath."

"By George!" said Myron Daw. "Who would have thought it of an honest doctor?"

IV

Jim Lee had come to the office of the "Star" in the flower of his wardrobe. His suit was pressed; his oxfords glowed a ruddy yellow; his tie was an embroidered madras brighter than the five-striped flag of China. He sat in a chair at one of Myron Daw's low windows, and in his long thin fingers held a brown fedora on his knees.

Across the room, with elbows on a case of head-line type, the doctor made a silent witness of the spectacle. Myron Daw was sitting in his arm-chair—reading in a clear, firm voice. A dusty book lay on the desk, with pages open. Jim Lee understood one word in every twenty.

"A truly magnificent specimen of vigorous growth," read Myron Daw, "is the Lady Ursula, with flowers large and synchronic, petals gracefully clustered; in dozens or in larger lots; delicately scented."

He stopped, and over the lenses of his spectacles looked sternly at Jim Lee; then turned the page and read again.

"No estate, however small, is complete without the decorative contribution of the dahlia. The species we have christened Glory of the Argonne blooms early; stiff wiry stems. If this sample has weak points we have so far failed to notice them."

Against the racks of coal-black type, the doctor shifted his position. The ceremony had continued for some ten or fifteen minutes. "Don't you think," he asked, "that we 've got far enough along for Mr. Lee to take the oath? If you can't find anything with longer words, I anticipate a disillusionment."

"Perhaps you 're right," said Myron Daw. He turned to the quiet Chinaman.

"Mr. Lee, I will say that for the present we 've not been able to secure you permission to enter a voting-booth. On election days Dr. Hodge or I will come personally for your ballot. You don't understand what I am saying; but you will, if you should ever want to vote. You will come now, if you please, and stand beside me."

Jim Lee caught "come," and crossed the room to his benefactor.

"You will raise your right hand, Mr. Lee."

The doctor translated this to action.

"You will repeat after me—as best you can," said Myron Daw, "the words I am now about to read you:

" 'Requires no pruning—our barberry—fastest growing plant—in cultivation.' "

With some help from the doctor, Jim contrived it. Myron Daw produced a button for his coat-lapel. They shook his hand. The smile never changed, but Jim Lee's eyes were shining when he left them.

"Say, Myron," said the doctor, "read that again about the barberry, will you? My wife 's been asking for something that would cover up the kitchen shed."

Months ago, this happened. Jim Lee is once more presiding over the shirts and cuffs of Myron Daw. If you should go into the laundry on Market Street to-morrow you would find that even though he worked in a tattered sweater a bright red, white, and blue button was pinned firmly to the cloth, above his breast-bone. It bears a blazing shield and two stern portraits:

"For President, William McKinley of Ohio—for Vice President, Garret A. Hobart of New Jersey."

PARSON TODD

I

THERE was a white board church in Vine Street from whose short steeple hung a high-voiced bell. The parsonage stood beside it: a patchwork of small rooms tacked on to one another at three levels. The dining-room arose two steps above the kitchen; the parlor fell across a precipice to make the hall. It was here that Anson Todd had brought his household goods: God's prophet on a salary no bricklayer would consider worth a minute's thought.

Hard times sat heavily upon the small estate that moldered in the shadow of the church. Hard times sat heavily upon the shoulders of its persevering tenant. He

225

was a threadbare man who had spent his
life at the short end of a fiscal problem: his
lean face like a hatchet with the blade along
his nose. But his eyes were friendly eyes—
his lips were ready for a smile. A church-
man of the older school, you might have
guessed if you had seen him; trained in his
trade before God took to bill-boards and
electric lights.

Fifty is not far beyond the prime of life.
That was about the mark that Anson Todd
had reached; but with the furrows on his
narrow face he looked impressively like
sixty-five. Slow, cautious, contemplative—
not many of his flock would have called him
"forceful"; yet there was one admirer to
whom he seemed a Galahad in shining armor.
That was his wife—a flurried little lady
who prefaced the slightest comment on her
own score with the byword, "As my hus-
bands says—" Popular, this Mrs. Todd--

despite a faculty for timing her few calls in Centerville society precisely at those moments when the stage was set for paying bridge scores at the rate of ten points to the penny.

Centerville thought Mrs. Todd a little plain, and more than a little unexciting—but liked her none the less. Certainly life had faced her with a poser. A house to steer along the brink of bankruptcy—four Todd youngsters to be educated, washed, and fed.

If the devil had taken her husband up the mountain, he might have pointed out a valley rich in bread.

II

It was customary for Anson Todd to face, on Sunday mornings, a church whose pews were two-thirds filled with worshipers in holiday regalia.

The church looked best in summer-time. Stained glass threw a ruddy light along the walls; the air was quiet, heavy; a bumblebee droned sleepily above the daisies in the summer hats. A pew would click, as some communicant endeavored stealthily to stretch his legs. Four vestrymen, in shoes that creaked like locomotive-brakes applied in haste, would watch their moment from the door. Having closed the windows twice, and opened them, they would wait impatiently for the collection. Now and then, in an unlucky moment, George Taylor's foot would slip—and the organ at whose bench he sat send out a toot of protest.

There would come a hymn, with the high voice of Mrs. Farley, who had taken singing-lessons, standing out above the rest. And in the lull that followed, Anson Todd would face his congregation from the pulpit.

"Brethren, I have chosen as my text to-day——"

He would lift his eyes from the Book before him, and send one look around the church: a gentle reminder to Fred Hoskins to stop coughing, and Mrs. Wilbur Matthews to have done with rustling in her seat and settle down.

"I have chosen as my text to-day the forty-first verse of the thirty-second chapter of Deuteronomy. Forty-first verse. Thirty-second chapter. Deuteronomy.

" 'If I whet my glittering sword, and mine hand take hold on judgment; I will render vengeance to mine enemies, and will reward them that hate me.' "

It was a favorite text. And a fiery sermon. Anson Todd's, if you remember, was the older school. He would invoke the Lord of Hosts, the God of Vengeance, the perils of hell-fire and damnation. He would whet the glittering sword, and swing it overhead—provided it was words.   But if you put the steel between his hands he might have beaten it to a plowshare.   He preached a soldier's sermon, and walked the earth a lamb.

For there was something of a gulf between these martial verses of the Old Testament, and life as Anson Todd himself had chosen to live it, here and now.   That did not prevent him from reaching back to these same verses for his sermons; it was characteristic of his faith, in fact, to find him there. For faith to Anson Todd was like his younger children's trousers: a venerable cloth retailored at the seams.   To certain simple concepts he adhered instinctively. He believed there was no section of the Scriptures not intended to be taken literally —that miracles were not parable but fact— not contrary to nature but superior to it;

that Man was modeled in the image of his Maker, but brought succeeding generations to disaster when he sold his birthright for an apple. More specifically, and in some ways a matter more decisive for his congregation, he was opposed to Sunday baseball, modern novels, and the modern dance; opposed to cards when played for money, though not when played for funds invested in a "prize."

As for that vast controversy between "science" and "religion" which had roiled far wider seas——

Distant eddies rippled into Centerville. Anson Todd deplored the issue; but if the issue should be forced he had no doubt that he must take his stand where his fathers stood before him. Religion would mean little less to him if he gave up Jonah and the whale; but give up Jonah, and who would follow next? Anson Todd was a sincere admirer of science; but he would have liked it better had it stuck to phonographs and electric lights—and not ventured so remotely from its field.

Still, it wasn't science that made him stop from time to time, and wonder where his work was taking him. He had another worry, more evasive.

III

They were planning an ice-cream social for the following Friday. It was an August night; and Anson Todd came home from a committee meeting, tired.

Half-past eight; three of the four young Todds were safely laid away in bed—the fourth within easy hailing-distance at the corner. Anson Todd found his wife in the kitchen, washing dishes, and hunted for a towel to help her at the sink.

"It all seems so *futile,* Sarah," he explained. "Sometimes it just comes over me with a sudden shock. You know. Things like this ice-cream business."

She was a quiet woman, Sarah Todd— presumably no hand to wrestle with an issue. Centerville had noted more than once that if she saw a penny on the floor, dropped there in the swift rush to make away with auction stakes before the door had opened for this unexpected caller, she seemed to take no notice. But for all her readiness to look past pennies, Sarah Todd had two keen eyes. This was not the first time her husband had proclaimed his desperation.

She took away from him the tea-pot with which his towel had made small progress, and told him more than likely he was tired.

He shook his head. It was n't that, he said.

She had no more to say until the kitchen

light was out, the eldest boy in bed, and two cane-seated chairs were rocking in the garden. "Were all your committee members at the meeting?"

"All of them? Of course they were!" he told her. "That's just the discouraging part of it. Let anything like an ice-cream social come along, and everybody's on the spot. It takes a 'party' of some sort to bring them.—Sarah, where did you put that fan? What's that?—Oh, yes. They'll come for a 'party' every time. But look at the church on Sundays. Never more than two-thirds full. And sometimes only half. And what sort of support do I get in the pulpit? I don't like to say it, Sarah. But you know as well as I do that there aren't a dozen people in the church who really follow what I say—follow, I mean, in the sense of wanting to have it out with me if they don't agree, or if they *do* agree have something more to say than 'Splendid sermon, parson.' It's these social affairs that stir them up. Picnics and the like. You take those amateur theatricals we had last month. More interest in them than in—well, in *Lent*. I wonder, Sarah. I wonder what we're heading for. I wonder what the church really means to all these people."

It wasn't the first time, as she'd observed; and she had noted that most times it went with tired nights in August or a touch of grippe in spring. Again, as she found the fan and volunteered to bring a pillow from the parlor, she suggested what she'd ventured more than once before.

Wasn't he expecting too much of people? In the pulpit, now. He'd said they didn't help him. But how could they? That was his job, there. Perhaps it was because it came *their* turn for action that they liked these picnics and these plays. Perhaps they did n't feel beyond their depth, the way they might have felt in arguments about religion, but had a sense of service to a "cause."

And sermons. All those Hebrew names were puzzling sometimes, even on her husband's lips. And did n't people always feel a little as if nothing much was expected of them, when they had no part to play?

She thought he overemphasized all that. His sermons were inspired. People told her that. She knew it in her heart. But the church— Was n't it a social center as much as anything, in these times when social ties were breaking up? Were n't chicken suppers as much a part of it as all the rest? Was n't it a church's business to give people circles they could move around in?

He shook his head. Picnics seemed a far cry from God's glory, he declared.

They sat in the darkness of the garden,

and in the path beneath the rockers of their chairs the gravel crunched.

"Do you think that 's cloud, or only haze?" asked Sarah Todd. "I hope it does n't rain and spoil the social."

IV

The lawn around the church was a fairy-land of paper lanterns dripping candle-wax on appetizing dishes down below. It did n't seem as if there ever were a spot so brightly lit before—so gay a Mecca as you cut across lots toward it, through the shadows. In and out between the white-topped tables streamed a friendly crowd. All Centerville had come to supper.

"Ice-cream bricks"—red, white, and green, in creamy stripes, laid pleasantly on paper doilies. Red and white were plain enough. Raspberry and vanilla. The green was always something of a puzzle.

Folding chairs and peppermints. Fragile soda-wafers. A sharp salt taste in every dish that came from ice-cream-freezer brine—young lovers eating with one spoon —the little girl who would n't eat the red, and traded with the small boy who did n't like vanilla. Hordes of summer bugs that swung around the lights in dizzy circles— to plunge at last, half stupified in their delight, to frozen death in saucers.

It was all there. This was a night of gladness. The ladies of the Choir Club, with gentlemen escorts at the freezers, rushed earnestly across the flaming lawn to wait on hungry tables.

And Parson Todd?

The heart and center of the party. Welcoming each guest as he arrived—encouraging the waitresses with a word of cheer—

helping churn the freezer. Imparting his condolences where condolences were due— congratulations for the lucky. Hunting for the missing spoon—ministering to the aged and infirm—rescuing a saucer from the baby.

"Anson!" His wife tried to stop him as he hurried past her with a plate.

"Just a minute, dear," he called to her. "Just wait until I get some more vanilla for Miss Parker."

A choir lady on a chair had lit another row of lanterns.

The church, behind the shadow of the hedge, looked down and caught the friendly gleam.

ERNEST LORING

I

THEY had n't taken the red cover off the fountain in the Public Square. It was late fall, and the goldfish were n't there, anyway. But if anything else had been left undone, Ben Cole declared he 'd like to know it. A mayor's committee had been appointed to meet the train, and covers were laid for thirty in the ball-room of the Grand Hotel. One of Centerville's most famous sons was coming home.

Sam Clark had been the first to hear the news. Sam was proprietor of the Grand Hotel, and had a telegram for rooms. "Coming for three days—Ernest Loring."

Ernest Loring coming home! The man

himself was just a name. Of course all
Centerville's old-timers remembered the
Loring family. They were early settlers
here; one Loring was the town's first
mayor. But they had moved away a generation back; and Ernest—destined to acquire
fame in later years—was a figure to be remembered vaguely. He was just a youngster at the time. Everybody knew that
somewhere he had learned to play the violin
—and years ago begun to get his picture in
the city papers. The magazines were always printing things about him now; but
it remained for Carter Hayes, who played
the organ in St. Mary's Church and kept
abreast of musical affairs, to measure the
full sweep of his achievement. This man,
he said, had played to royalty in London,
Rome, and Budapest. He had packed the
concert-halls in a dozen cities, and swept
the press by storm. Critics showered him

with praise; people paid him as much as six or seven hundred dollars for an hour's song. "That sounds like him," agreed Sam Clark. "I 've got to take the bed and wash-stand out of No. 6, I guess. He says he wants a 'sitting-room.' Next thing you know, he 'll be asking for a private bath."

Ernest Loring coming home: and as the rumor spread, a score of witnesses came to the front with long-forgotten memories. Everybody knew the old Loring House on Vine Street. Marlin Day, the postman, could remember a small boy forever playing on the jews'-harp when he got there with the mail. Grandpa Gilpin, the more he thought of it, was sure he 'd held the lad upon his knee and let him listen to the ticking of his watch. Harvey Peeke could recall a pale-faced youngster in the old stone chapel on McDonough Street, who used to sit beside the organist and pump the bellows. That would be Ernest, the town agreed. No doubt he got his inspiration Sunday mornings.

Centerville, it was admitted on all sides, had good reason to be proud. It had shaped a youth, and sent him forth to conquer. Here he was, returning with the tribute of his years. In certain quarters there had been a rush for Harley's music store, and a good deal of satisfaction with results. Not only was Ernest Loring represented on these disks of brittle wax; his records, it was noted with approval, cost as much as any artist's on the boards. "A dollar more than the sextette from Lucia," averred Ben Cole, with civic pride. "And that's got six of them a-going it at once."

It was a little disappointing, though, Ben admitted to his wife, to find a Loring opus on both faces. "Oh, I like it well enough," he volunteered. "I can see how royalty in

Europe would take to it like ducks. Never heard a fellow fiddle faster on those high notes in my life. But I should think they 'd put a light sketch on the other side. You know. Sort of break the tension."

For a guest of Loring's talent, everybody thought, the town had nothing musical to offer. Barbour's band would meet the train; but there was no use thinking of a concert. "He 'd be tired of music, anyway," Sam Clark declared. "Think of having to play a concert six or seven times a week!" It was decided, however, that Centerville would show it took an interest in things musical if some minor touch were added here; Myra Keyts, who at twelve could play Liszt's "Liebestraum" without the music and Grieg's "An den Frühling" if somebody turned the pages for her, would be dressed in pink and white to play at the

banquet while coffee-cups were being filled.
For the rest, there would be a welcome at
the station—he would come on No. 8—that
made the best connections with the west;
there would be some sort of morning celebration, Tuesday, under the auspices of the
Oratorio Society, and a drive through down-
town streets to show him how the place had
grown; Wednesday would come a dance
and a reception; Thursday they would take
him to the train, and send him on his way
with some appropriate gift.

All this, of course—provisionally. Everybody knew that Musicians are a baf-
fling lot who go around with neckties off and
overturn the best-laid plans. Sam Clark
was ready for a wager that not one item
on the program would be carried out.

Ben Cole declared he would n't be surprised to see the man arrive with hair around

his shoulders—and hoped that he was right.

The town looked forward to the eccentricity of genius.

II

Ernest Loring sat at the head of the horseshoe table in the Grand Hotel, and told himself this first-night banquet was a failure.

To be sure, it was with no thought of banquets he had come to Centerville. It is fair to say that he had not foreseen himself a public guest. The telegram for reservations, to which he owed this demonstration in his honor, had been despatched on grounds of prudence: early memories of the Grand Hotel suggesting that with two rooms reserved instead of one, he stood a double chance of sleeping somewhere else than straight above the kitchen. He had looked forward to three quiet days. There would

be the town to see—he had n't been back
once in thirty years; there would be the
old house with a double-decker porch that
used to make a gallant steamboat, and
the Grove Street School, and a much admired colleague in the theft of neighbors'
cherries, now remembered as a certain
"Whitey"; there would be a respite from the
routine of a minstrel's life, and—who knows?
—perhaps a chance or two of bringing down
a quail; Glover's Woods, they used to say,
was full of them.

That was yesterday. To-night, quail and
a quiet holiday seemed lost beyond retriev-
ing. From the moment he had heard the
martial strains of a triumphant band—and
beheld, on looking through the window of
his train, a broad linoleum banner holding
to the sky a giant "Welcome" followed
by his name—Ernest Loring had abandoned
Centerville as he had planned it. Still—it

was theirs to choose. He was the prodigal, home once more for a paternal blessing. But need the blessing show—he looked around the table at these thirty banquet guests—so early in his stay the marks of frost-bite?

Myra Keyts had played Liszt's "Liebe-straum." He had done his best to give her an ovation. But the spirits of the company drooped as unmistakably as the yellow heads of Mr. Clark's uneaten celery; and he had abandoned the effort as beyond his power. From the first oyster through the salad course he had had to struggle for each bit of conversation like a man at sea, in a heavy swell, at a tableful of listless diners. The evening, clearly, was a fizzle.

Coffee-cups were cleared away. Smoke arose from the thin tips of native panetelas.

The party broke up at nine thirty.

Ten minutes later Ernest Loring's thirty hosts were putting on their coats and over-shoes in Sam Clark's down-stairs lobby.

"Nice fellow, eh?"

"Yes, darned nice fellow.   Not quite what I expected, though."

"Nor me."

"I thought those violinists always wore a long black tie."

"And hair, you know—down here.   My wife said sure he'd have his hair down here."

"I know.   Certainly does n't look like a musician, does he?"

"Say, what impressed *me* was the way he did n't do a thing unusual.   You know—the way they say those fellows always do."

"I know. My wife was telling me— 'You wait,' she said, 'just wait until you see him! You 've never seen a genius. You never know what they 're going to wear, or what they 'll say, or what they 're up to next.' I thought he'd raise a row or something."

"Say! he might have been a banker from Chicago."

III

It turned out, in the end, that Centerville was right. A genius is a genius. There 's no dodging it.

Funny, they admitted later, the way nobody noticed it that first night. There it was: as plain as the headlight on a railway train—and yet nobody had the wit to see it. But then, the thing was so completely unexpected.—The plain fact was that genius never took a more amazing turn than in the fellow Loring: here he was—fresh from triumphs in a dozen fields, imbued with the

capricious skill that made him one man in
a hundred thousand—and yet so odd a prank
had genius played that it left him just like
everybody else.

There was his interest in the town, for
instance. No one had thought he 'd have a
moment's time for sights the ordinary guest
was always shown; things like Jordan Park
and the high-school gym and the refrigerating-plant of Bunn & Company. What
were small affairs like these for a man who 'd
seen the world from Budapest to California
—and had an artist's temperament, to boot?
He would n't look at them; or, if he did,
he 'd jeer.—Far from it. So odd was this
eccentric man that when it came to seeing
sights of the sort a traveling salesman
might write home about, he never tired. He
raced three boys through Jordan Park.
He took a picture of the high-school gym.
He crawled so far beneath the pipes of Bunn

& Company's refrigerating-plant, to see the place it froze the hardest, that they had to send a Bunn & Company mechanic in to steer him out again.

There is no accounting for the tricks of talent; for a violinist, Ernest Loring was an odd one. He took an interest in the traffic laws, and argued with Sam Clark about the chalk-marks painted on the curb where Market Street cuts Maple. He learned that Lewisburg, six miles up-stream along the river, was famous as a place for making glass; and, when they 'd taken him by motorcar, brought home with him a glass carnation. He went to Mrs. Nesbit's dinner and amazed her guests with his insistence all hands present play charades. He dropped in one afternoon at Elmer Bradley's billiard-rooms, and pocketed a triple carom.

And then there was the evening with the violin.

Centerville knew the rules. When the tight-rope artist dines with you, you don't invite him to the family clothes-line after dinner. There are certain covenants of hospitality. But Centerville, without much confidence in music on its own score, would have liked to say that it had heard this genius on his violin. It did n't ask him. It knew the rules. But suddenly, that last evening at the dance given in his honor at the Woodmen's Hall, he had appeared from nowhere with a fiddle on his shoulder. And even as John Barbour, on the platform, silenced his band with the quick beat of a baton that had the reverence of a roadside minstrel for a master, he had caught the slow Hawaiian tune before it touched the floor and tossed it to the ceiling. Softly, at first—with a beat of his foot and a nod of his head, as if to urge the crowd to keep on dancing; then with syncopation such as Barbour's band had never dreamed, as he caught the threadbare rhythm on his bow and spun it through a thousand variations.

He stopped. And while the dancers paused, forgetting the applause that always ends each dance in Centerville, he drew his bow across the strings again. No dance, this time. Nor anything Ben Cole had struggled to pronounce, when his wife came home with Loring records. But tunes that stole as softly from his shoulder as dawns steal in from sea. Pickaninny songs, and snatches of a hoarse voice on the Volga—hymns that of a sudden sounded far away from choir-stalls and in the hills somewhere, immeasurably at peace—bits of headstrong passion from an unknown East that seemed to make the tom-toms beat as nautch-girls danced around the fires, stamping to the rumble as it gathered speed.

That was all.   They put him aboard his train next day.   He had promised to come back again: "We're neighbors, now." They cheered him, when the train pulled out—and felt that they surrendered to a wider fame the affections of a well-loved son.

There is no doubt about the eccentricities of great musicians.   The Oratorio Society still talks of Ernest Loring and his unexampled ways.

PETER QUIGLEY

I

IF faith is there, the rest is easy. That is the way the young son of Martin Quigley saw the two-horned bear.

You must remember that this happened on a very special day, when children danced along the curb and all the shops in town had posters pasted on the window-panes and from a hundred pudgy hands balloons went bobbing in the air. Banners flying in the breeze—shouts of salesmen hawking whips and whistles, ice-cream molded into cones. Earth new-turned; young spring, once more; and circus.

At midday, in the bright glare of a May sun, the crowd on Market Street was waiting restlessly. This was Peter Quigley's first adventure. He was six. There had n't been a circus come to town for several years. He stood, now, very near the curb, with his hand clasped in his mother's, and beat back a slowly mounting fear that something had happened to the largest of the elephants, and that after all this waiting the parade would never come. He was a mite of a boy, with a sailor hat which he detested and a sailor suit which pleased him with its trousers pockets. He had dreamed for nights of tigers that stood on their black and yellow legs to open kitchen windows and come climbing through. He had found, no longer ago than yesterday, two large black footprints near the chicken-coop, and confided to his father, at the breakfast-table, that in his judgment this could only mean a grizzly bear.

Too young, this small Peter, to share in

the adventure of dressing by starlight to
meet the circus at the train; but there were
other pleasures of anticipation not denied
him. Bill-boards, for example. For weeks
the high fence behind the Baptist Church
and the brick walls of Graham's grocery had
been the habitat of every creature that sur-
vived the flood in Noah's Ark. Lions.
Tigers. Zebras. A buffalo or two. A
wild boar with head erect, tusks bristling.
Brumbaugh Brothers' One and Only Greatest Show on Earth had samples of them all.
And from four corners of the poster, four
Brumbaughs looked with pride.   John, Ed,
Dan, and Bert: each labeled with his name,
cheeks tinted with a bill-board red.   Which
brother's job was which, had been a much-
debated question in the rank of Peter's
friends.   Dan looked the fiercest: he would
be the one who cracked the lion's whip.
Bert wore a cockade in his hat: of course he

rode the horses round the ring. Ed was stern but a little sleepy: he might have trained those great black hulks that looked like elephants but went, on bill-boards, by the name of Pachyderms. John was the least impressive of the four. It had been decided, in the end, that John would take the tickets.

Four Brumbaugh brothers. And four weeks to wait. All that was over now. Peter Quigley stood at his mother's side, and felt the heavy hand of Fate. For two hours there had been shouts of "Here it comes!"— each shout attended by swift dashes from the curb, to see—with mothers snatching children back to safety from the street and wails of anguish over one or two escaped balloons. There were more shouts now. But they would shout in vain. "It won't come," Peter Quigley whispered to his mother. "It won't come. You see."

But this time, back of all the shouts, was something new and strange. Somewhere, Peter Quigley knew, a railway-engine was escaping from the tracks and playing sudden tunes. "The cally-ope! The cally-ope!" the boys were shouting. "It's coming. You can hear the cally-ope!" And even before Peter, tugging at his mother's hand, could be rewarded with a definition which he felt to be his due—of this new phenomenon not once referred to, on the bill-boards—the pageant of the Brumbaugh Brothers swept in view: ladies with white plumes and velvet suits, on horseback— a band astride a wagon-top—a clown who drove a donkey-cart and scattered paper favors—a tank, two eyes: "Look, Peter! there's the hippopotamus!"—more clowns —a troupe of cowboys—a polar bear, not very fierce, it's true, who swung his long thin head left-right, right-left, left-right, as if he ran on clockwork—another band—a lion on his back, indifferent to this splendid chance to growl—a string of wary elephants who held each other by a small amount of tail, and hurried on with little mincing steps like old men on an ice-pond.

Peter Quigley watched the last of it go by, and sighed. He would see the circus in the afternoon: that had been promised from the start. But it was hard to come back from a world of dreams achieved to common earth again. "Mother!" he gave her hand a sudden tug. "I want to ask you something."

The crowd was breaking up. His mother seemed to have no time for answers. They must hurry, if they meant to get there early in the afternoon. She 'd have to cook some sort of meal before they started. Friendly, but impatient to be on its way, the crowd went jostling up the street.

"Peter! Don't lag that way. Stay closer to mother."

A little girl of Peter's age was shrieking to her sister. "He waved at me. Right straight at me. The clown did."

They passed a man who said he'd never seen a fiercer tiger.

"Don't lag now, Peter."

"Mother," he panted, out of breath. "I want to ask you something."

"Wait till you get home."

"Mother, some of those cages had board covers on the sides."

"All right. Come hurry now."

"But why?"

"I don't know. Because they didn't want you to look in."

"Then what did they bring them for?"

"Oh, I don't know. To make you curious, I suppose. If you saw everything the first time, you wouldn't want to go this afternoon. They keep the best ones hidden."

Peter pondered to the corner.

"The best ones, mother?"

"I suppose so."

"Better than the lion?"

"I suppose so."

"Better than two lions?"

"I suppose so."

"Better than three lions?"

"Don't ask questions when mother's in a hurry, Peter. You 'll see it all this afternoon."

Peter meant to see the equal of three lions, or know the reason why.

II

To young eyes it was a scene of giant splendor.

They had filled a small tin pail with fil-

tered water, for the afternoon—and bundled
three pillows from the parlor sofa. The
seats were hard, his mother said. There
had been some sort of luncheon in the kitchen. But Peter could n't eat. Filled up,
he told his mother. Too much taffy, his
father said; but Peter knew that what he
tasted was his heart. Hours, it seemed to
take his mother to find her parasol and snap
the latches on the window-screens. Then
an endless wait before they had a chance
to crowd aboard a trolley-car. And at last
the circus-ground: transformed by magic
overnight. Here, where only yesterday a
boy like Peter might have rolled in grass
waist-high—and never dreamed that para-
dise on earth existed—great cliffs of canvas
had been flung against the sky: the whole
earth peopled with engaging creatures.

Small tents first: mere outposts to the
great white tabernacle where the band was

drumming out a march. Peter, hurrying
on, one hand in either parent's, caught swift
glimpses of new games: booths where men
were tossing rings at rows of canes—more
booths where other men were shooting with
real guns at little pasteboard rabbits that
ran past and seemed to die, only to return
again; all sorts of fascinating treasures
dangling at the end of strings: paper knives
and bright enamel vases, kewpie dolls and
round glass balls with butterflies inside.

Ten cents to shoot a rifle. Five cents to
ring a cane. But where the crowd was
thicker, and his father swung him shoulder-
high, were pleasures rarer and more costly.
There the side-show hung its vivid posters on
a canvas wall: Educated Horses who could
count to nine and pick out colors faster
than their masters; wild men from Darkest
Africa; dancers from the Khedive's Pal-
ace—arms poised high above their heads,

jewels flashing on their throats: an early morning scene, as Peter's quick eye told him, before these ladies (doubtless lion-tamers) had had a chance to comb their hair and dress.

Not a bad idea, Peter's father said, to stop a moment, go inside, and rest.

Peter thought that very strange. Why any one should want to waste time watching horses count to nine, when there were lions just beyond, he could n't understand. Neither, it seemed, could Peter's mother.

"The idea!" she observed.

They moved on to the gateway of Valhalla.

III

From a perch half-way to the eaves of Brumbaugh Brothers' biggest tent, with the shells of peanuts sifting down from overhead and the hot smell of circus in the air, Peter Quigley watched the panorama with bright eyes. He was thrilled; no doubt of that. But not even the Thundering, Desperate, and Furious Four-Horse Roman Chariot-Race filled his cup of pleasure to the brim. He made no secret of the fact that here, before the show was over, would come wonders greater still.

It had started, first, with a triumphant march led by the band and trailing at its end a float of ladies armed with shields and spears: America, the program said, Receiving Homage from the Nations. Peter was less impressed by that than by the Acrobatic Averys—"positively all one family of father, mother, five daughters, and one son" —who leaped into the center ring the moment it was cleared. Here was action with no stop for catching breath. The father had small patience with his daughters. He would stamp his feet in a box of sand, bark once, and clap his hands. Like reindeer flying from the hounds his family would race across the ring and leap upon his shoulders. Peter did not wish to be unjust. He knew that his own father was a noble man. No one could make a better whistle with a stick of willow and a knife. Still, there was something splendid here; perhaps his father's shoulders had n't always been so thin. "Daddy, could *you* do that before you married mother?"—One clap. And with a mighty heave the father of the Avery family sent his children flying to the farthest corners of the ring.

They turned upon him for a new assault: he stamped his feet in the box of sand to show how little all that troubled him. He would meet them head on, this time, and bent his shoulders for the charge. But whether they bore him to earth, or whether he stood them off a second time, Peter Quigley had no chance to see. He had discovered, of a sudden, that this great colosseum had three rings—and used them with an utter disregard of whether any one was looking! All this time—it had never occurred to him that they could waste their treasures this way—Ring No. 1 had been resounding with the barks of bears who rode velocipedes; all this time, on a never-quiet perch above Ring No. 3, Mlle. Daisy de la Marne had been swinging from one heel and then the other: and now, while the band marked time, and the snare-drum worked its way from a slow start to a shrill reverberating rattle, she flipped herself through space to turn four dozen somersaults before she hit the net below.

It was discouraging, thought Peter. Not

only must you be content with what little
you could see by not looking somewhere else
you wanted to: the whole thing moved so
swiftly it was certain to be finished hours in
advance of supper-time. Men in baggy
trousers ran to knot and unknot ropes.
Whistles blew. They snatched the Bengal
tigers from their cage before they had a
chance to show their willingness to eat their
trainer.

It was wonderful enough. Peter Quigley had n't eyes enough to look at half of
what he treasured. But it moved so fast it
took your breath away.

And then, though he 'd been waiting for
it from the very first, it seemed they never
once revealed the thing most wonderful of
all. He knew it. Perhaps, with all these
people here, it was n't safe. And still——

Peter Quigley tugged his father's coat-
sleeve. It was now or never.

IV

The last of the acrobats had left off scrambling one another round the ring. Overhead the slack wire still whipped gently from the leaps and bounds of slippered toes. The crowd was making for the exits.

"Father, when we get outside—when we get outside you take me to see something, will you?"

"What is it, Peter?"

"It's something."

"Where?"

"It's in a cage."

"Now, Peter," his mother said, behind them. "You've seen the cages now. It's almost supper-time."

"But you *told* me, mother."

"What, Peter?"

"You told me I could see this afternoon."

They were on the ground again. The

steep rows of shaky seats had meant slow progress. "What's he talking about?" asked Peter's father.

"Goodness only knows," his mother said. "You'd think he'd be satisfied and not ask questions after all he's seen."

Too late. Too late, thought Peter. He would never see it now.

"What was it, son?" his father asked.

"Oh, father in those covered cages!"

"What covered cages, Peter?"

"Those ones they had this morning in the street."

"*I* know what he wants," his mother said. "Some of the wagons were boarded up in the parade. I told him he could see what was in them when he came this afternoon."

Just that, thought Peter. "Why can't I, father?"

"But you have, Peter," his father said. "I took you through the whole menagerie before the circus started. Don't you remember? Were n't all the covers off the cages?"

So that 's the way they meant to fool him! First pretend they did n't know. And then pretend there was n't anything to see. He shook his head. "I saw two of them behind a little tent."

"Two wagons?"

"Yes."

"Are those the ones you want to see?"

He nodded. "Oh, father! you know that place I spilled the ink spots on the carpet? I won't ever spill them there again. And I won't whisper, and I don't care if you don't give me a penny for the candy store, and I 'll always go up-stairs to bed. Please, father. Please."

"Why not?" His father was talking to Peter's mother now. "It 's just a step or two. You wait across the street."

"Just *silly,* I call it," his mother said.

"Most boys would be more grateful for the things they 've seen."

But Peter trailed along behind his father. Not that tent. A littler one. Tired? Not a bit. "They may be gone," his father said. "Oh, no." But Peter's courage failed him. "This tent?" The next beyond. Around behind, they were. Two big green wagons— Ah!

Heart beating like a hammer, Peter let his father lift him up. Huge wagons, of a brilliant green—with mountain torrents dashing down their sides. One small window at the forward end: screened with heavy netting. Peter held his breath, and peered inside.

And shall it be recorded that in one of them he saw two piles of well-coiled rope— and in the other one, a bushel of potatoes?

No, better to let Peter paint the scene himself, as he described it to the two small Bradley boys that evening.

"He had the zebra in his hands. The bear did. He was eating supper. His fur was awful. My father said the boards were made of iron so he could n't eat them through. He's worse than any lion. My mother says he's worse than two of them. And maybe three. The bears *you* saw were n't anything. This bear is the only kind like him in all the world. He's got two horns. He's the worst one in the circus. That's why they shut him up. So little boys like you won't be afraid. It's only big boys six years old who can look at him. Freddy is his name."

If faith is there, the rest is easy. Peter's father, if the truth be known, had to hold fast lest the iron boards give way and a two-horned bear partake of human flesh for supper.